ABLE AN EXECUTIONER SERIES
TEAM

Justice by Fire

Dick Stivers

D0441919

A GOLD EAGLE BOOK FROM
W RLDWIDE

TORONTO • NEW YORK • LONDON • PARIS
AMSTERDAM • STOCKHOLM • HAMBURG
ATHENS • MILAN • TOKYO • SYDNEY

First edition August 1983

ISBN 0-373-61207-9

Special thanks and acknowledgment to
G.H. Frost for his contributions to this work.

Printed in Canada

1

Roberto Quesada, commander of *El Ejercito de los Guerreros Blancos*, greeted the young Salvadorans with handshakes and *abrazos*, the Latin American embrace of macho friendship.

Each of the six young men—all wide-shouldered, with the close-cut hair and straight posture of soldiers—spoke for a moment with their commander, then filed through the double-door entry of the ultramodern Miami mansion of concrete and plate glass.

Quesada followed the last man through the doorway, as the limousine drivers unloaded suitcases from the trunks of the Lincolns and Cadillacs parked on the circular driveway.

Across Ocean Avenue, in a rental car parked in the night shadow of a flowering silk tree, a reporter braced a motorized Nikon on the car's steering wheel. He scanned the mansion's windows. Dwarf palms and ferns screened the interior from his sight. Finally, he took his eye from the camera's viewfinder. He watched the chauffeurs carry suitcases inside. Snapping the cap onto the 400mm telephoto lens, Floyd "The Cat" Jefferson carefully set down the camera. He noted the time and exposure details in his notebook: 9:38 P.M. Color Kodak 1000 ASA.

He checked a schedule of airline flights. The evening flight from El Salvador had arrived in Miami less than an hour earlier. Floyd Jefferson knew the six soldiers came from El Salvador. To double-check his assumption, he worked out the crosstown travel time from the airport, added time to clear customs. El Salvador.

Who're they here to kill? Or perhaps they are here only to talk about murder. And torture and mutilation.

Parked a mere hundred yards from the leader of one of El Salvador's most feared death squads, Jefferson leaned back on the car seat to wait. He wanted more photos. Even with the high-speed emulsion of the film and the camera's expensive optics, night photography of subjects in motion remained an exercise in luck. He had the good luck of the entryway lighting illuminating the Salvadorans' faces, but any detail—a wrong guess on the exposure, a flare off the windshield, the turn of a head—might ruin a photo. His story required at least one good shot of every member of the death squad. Perhaps he would not learn why they had come to Miami, but he could prove they came.

Soon, Jefferson would introduce the North American public to the *Guerreros Blancos*—the White Warriors. North Americans already knew of the Salvadoran death squads terrorizing that nation in the name of anti-Communism. Everyone who owned a television had seen—in lurid color—the bloated, decomposing corpses of students, nurses, teachers and farmers dumped in the ditches and the ravines of El Salvador. Forty thousand civilians had been murdered in the campaign of terror to defeat the Salvadoran government's attempts to reform and modernize the country.

But the news of one murder—only one man hacked to death, beheaded with machetes—would carry the name of the Army of White Warriors to every citizen of the United States and Canada. Soon, with photos and details and sworn testimony, Jefferson would take the first step on the road of protest.

He had no illusions. There would be no trials of the murderers, not in El Salvador nor in the United States. The American administration went through the twice yearly charade of "human rights" certification. Every six months, the United States Congress and Senate protested the thousands of murders, including eight United States citizens, but noted for the record that the number of murders per night continued to decline. Then the representatives of the people of the United States of America voted to provide more money and weapons for *los escuadrones de muerte*, the squadrons of death.

Despite his hatred and the horror of what he had seen, Jefferson laughed to himself. Damn right they're not killing as many. That place is running out of people to kill.

They had hacked his friend to death. Jefferson knew he could not force a trial of the killers, not even an arrest, but the journalists and camera crews would crowd the iron gateway of Quesada's Miami Beach sanctuary. Quesada would face microphones and photographers every time he left his estate. After a few days of that, perhaps the Salvadoran mass murderer would return to his own country.

Where he could get shot . . . .

A car passed. Fear touched Jefferson when he saw the driver look at him. He glanced in the rearview mirror. The car continued south, toward the lights of the towering tourist hotels at the other end of the island. He saw no one walking on the asphalt or on the tree-shadowed sidewalks. He scanned the fronts of the nearest estates. No guards watched him.

At the Quesada mansion, the chauffeurs waited, standing in a group behind one of the Lincolns. A butane lighter flared. Cigarettes scratched arcs against the darkness as men gestured. Jefferson watched the windows of the mansion.

Why did the drivers wait? Jefferson had seen them carry suitcases into the house. If Quesada's gang planned to stay with their commander, why the waiting limousines? Did they intend to tour Miami's nightspots?

Jefferson totaled the numbers. Quesada and his wife and four children occupied the mansion. Plus four bodyguards and a live-in maid. Now six guests. A total of seventeen.

Unless Quesada had installed racks of bunk beds, the six young men would sleep at a hotel. Then why had the chauffeurs carried in suitcases?

Tires screeched to a halt. A light blinded Jefferson. He heard car doors fly open, slam shut. Careful not to move too quickly, he sat up straight as he put both hands on the dashboard, fingers wide.

"What you doing here, boy?" a voice demanded. From the curb side, a flashlight swept over the interior of the car.

"Nothing, officer, nothing at all."

"Then tell me why you're doing nothing *here*."

"Have I broken a law, officer?"

The second patrolman opened the passenger-side door. "Don't get lippy, punk. You don't belong in this neighborhood. Out."

"Leaving right now."

"Out of the car!"

"Yes, officer. I'm getting out. Don't shoot."

"Shut your mouth!" the second patrolman ordered.

"What's your name?" demanded the first police officer. "What're you doing with all this photographic equipment?"

Jefferson managed to leave the car without lowering his hands. He stood on the sidewalk, hands clasped behind his head. The radio of the Dade County Police cruiser blared numbers and addresses into the warm, humid quiet of the luxury district. A slight ocean breeze brought the scents of brine and jasmine.

"Why aren't you answering, boy?"

"I'm twenty-three years old, sir."

"I didn't ask how old you are. Show us some identification."

"Yes, sir. Reaching for my identification. Here it is, sir."

"Take it out of the wallet."

"Keep your hands up!"

Jefferson raised his hands above his head as he slipped his California driver's license out of his wallet. He held out the license above the officer's head.

"You think you're funny?"

"No, sir. I don't think I'm funny. You told me to

keep my hands up. My hands are up. You asked me for my name, you told me to shut up—''

"We got ourselves a California black, here. From foggy San Francisco. So, you explain to me, California boy. What are you doing here? This is an exclusive neighborhood. What do you want?''

"A tan. I heard about the Florida sunshine—''

"Down. Push-up position! Feet wide. Hands wide.''

As Floyd Jefferson stared at the seashell-patterned sidewalk inches from his nose, headlights flashed past. Another limousine swept through the gates of Quesada's mansion. Jefferson watched the entry. He thought he saw two Anglo faces pass through the entry's lights, one man with close-cut gray hair, another with blond hair.

"Eyes down!'' One of the policemen put his shoe on Jefferson's back to force his face into the concrete. "What is it you're looking over there for, boy?''

The other officer read Jefferson's name and San Francisco address into the radio. "It says he's a reporter. He's out here on Ocean Avenue, taking pictures. What of, he won't say.''

Listening to the patrolman broadcast his identity and profession into the Florida night, Jefferson felt a formless, irrational fear touch his imagination. He thought of police-band scanners and of the thousands of expatriate Cubans employed at every level in the Miami city government. As his imagination threatened to turn his dread into panic, he reassured himself with the knowledge that in a few hours he would return to the West Coast, far from the Salvadorans and Cubans and uniformed bigots of Miami.

Days later, Jefferson would laugh at the naive thought that distance might protect him.

After all, airlines sold tickets to anyone who had the money.

2

In the next apartment, Lucha Villa sang of love and loss from a radio tuned to a Tijuana station. The Rivera family gathered around the table as David Holt spread typed sheets and legal papers in front of Antonio Rivera. An attorney with a lucrative practice in San Francisco, Holt wore the gray-suit uniform of an advocate. Though also an attorney, Señor Rivera wore khaki work pants and a polyester shirt. His hands bore the blisters and torn skin of a professional who now earned his living by manual labor.

A month before, Señor Rivera had served as mayor of a tiny town in the Salvadoran province of Sonsonate. Now he, his wife and their surviving children hid in a one-room apartment in a San Diego barrio. By day, he cleared brush and broke concrete, while his wife Lidia taught their children English with the aid of comic books and television soap operas. Nights, they flipped through the television channels for news of their country.

Day and night, they watched the street for Immigration. They feared deportation to El Salvador more than death. If the United States Department of Immigration and Naturalization Service seized the family and returned them to El Salvador, they would suffer the same horror that had taken their teenage son: death by mutilation, courtesy of the knives and machetes of *El Ejercito de los Guerreros Blancos*.

"We can prepare a petition proving your fear of persecution if you are deported," Holt told Señor and Señora Rivera, "but the State Department refuses to recognize Salvadorans as political refugees. First, we must have irrefutable proof of the political terrorism directed against your family—"

Rivera touched the envelope containing the black-and-white photos of his murdered son and his administrative aide. Only sixteen years old, his son had died in the courtyard of the family's home. Farmers had found the remains of his aide in a ditch. The Riveras never looked at the photos. To show Holt, they had handed him the envelope, then turned their eyes away as he studied the nauseating horror.

"The photos are not enough—"

"And the notes from the *Guerreros Blancos*...." Rivera touched the clear plastic that sheathed the blood-marked pages the death squad had left on the bodies. In the stilted Spanish of a university graduate, the notes declared the young Rivera a Communist and an enemy of El Salvador.

"And the articles from the North American and European newspapers," Rivera continued, gesturing at the thick bundle of clippings reporting the murder of Ricardo Marquez, the San Francisco journalist.

"The murder is the foundation of your case. First, we must prove it happened as you say. The Salvadoran authorities claim the Communists killed Mr. Marquez. They claim you arranged the murder. We may in fact need to fight requests to extradite you to face a trial in a Salvadoran court. If we can somehow prove the death squad committed the murder, and that you witnessed it, we will have a good case for asylum. If not...perhaps we can gather public support for your case. However, the State Department does not recognize rallies and slogans in court."

"But he was an American," Señor Rivera protested. "*Los Blancos* murdered him. Doesn't your government want justice? Do they not want to protect the rights of their own citizens?"

Holt shook his head, no. "They will not admit his death was murder. The State Department told the press and the Marquez family that he died in a cross fire, an accident of war."

"Machine guns that shoot machete bullets—" Rivera laughed bitterly. "I saw the *Blancos* kill Ricardo. I saw them take his head and put it on a fence post. I told your embassy of what I saw. I identified the *Blancos*. Then they came to kill my family. Your country is a democracy. You elect your leaders. How can your people elect leaders who lie and deceive and betray?"

The San Francisco attorney struggled to answer, his lips forming the first syllable of a rational and educated explanation of his president's and nation's Central American policies. But his voice died before he spoke. He knew no rational explanation for the parody of foreign policy his nation's leaders presented to the world: the circus parade of ignorance and fictions, and the vainglorious leading democracy to defeat in the undeclared war against the Soviet empire.

Footsteps stopped at the door. A knock sounded,

saving the North American attorney from voicing his own despair.

Señora Rivera answered the door, opening it only a few inches. "Who are you? What do you want?"

"I'm Floyd Jefferson. Mr. Holt told me to come here—"

"Floyd!" Holt ushered the young black reporter into the crowded apartment.

"I would've called but your office couldn't give me a number."

"You have the photos?"

Jefferson passed an envelope to Holt. "Got on the plane as soon as I got them from the lab."

The attorney introduced the aspiring journalist to the Riveras. "Floyd Jefferson worked with Ricardo. Now he's working with us. Mayor Rivera, Mrs. Rivera—"

The young man surprised them with Spanish. *"Mucho gusto, señor. Señora. Lo siento por las problemas mi país da ustedes. Antes del muerte de mi amigo Ricardo, pienso...."* When he paused to think of the correct Spanish phrase, Señor Rivera cut off the apology.

"You are not responsible. Please, we speak in English, so we are not rude to Mr. Holt. Did you study Spanish in college?"

Jefferson laughed. "No, I studied English. I talked Spanish with my mother."

They sat around the table. "Your mother spoke Spanish?" Señora Rivera asked.

"She came from Puerto Rico. My dad spoke some Spanish, too. And Indian. And Gaelic. He came from New Mexico."

"You have many bloods," Señor Rivera commented. "Truly a child of America."

"I got a *lot* of different people in me—black, white, red, maybe yellow." Jefferson laughed. "When people call me black, I want to set them straight, 'Nah, rainbow.' *Niño del arco iris*."

Holt stopped the small talk. "Floyd has just returned from Miami. Look at these photos. Perhaps...."

Despite the low light and forced development, the prints captured every feature and expression of the Salvadorans. Holt spread the eight-by-ten blowups across the table's pink Formica. Señor Rivera pointed to one young Salvadoran.

"This one. He was one of the soldiers who killed Mr. Marquez. This man—" he pointed to the photo of the death-squad commander "—I have seen him in the newspapers. A colonel, I believe."

"Roberto Quesada," Holt informed him. "Ex-colonel Quesada. He resigned his army commission in December 1979—"

Señor Rivera nodded. "Yes, after the first junta."

"He opposed the voting rights and land reforms," Holt continued. "Now he directs the Army of White Warriors from Miami—"

"Why does your Immigration not deport him?" Señora Rivera asked.

"'Cause he's a rich man," Jefferson answered.

"Do you recognize any of the others?" Holt asked the Riveras.

"Perhaps this one...." Señora Rivera picked up one photo. "I think... I think maybe I saw him in the village. But... I cannot be sure."

Señor Rivera waved a hand over the photos. "Why do we look at these? They do not show what happened that day. Pictures from Miami prove nothing."

"If we can link Quesada to the murder, if Quesada gave the order from Miami to murder Ricardo Marquez in Sonsonate, he is then subject to prosecution under the laws of the United States," Holt said. "And for the period of the investigation and trial, you and your family will receive protection as witnesses."

"And perhaps we will not. Perhaps they will come to kill us. If I had not called your embassy in San Salvador, my son would be alive. Now you want us to trust your justice?"

"Yes. I want you to trust our laws. In the United States, no one is above the law. Not even wealthy colonels."

"Not even the White House?" Señora Rivera asked.

Holt repeated his words. "No one is above the law. The law protects us all."

"In El Salvador, there are many laws," muttered Señor Rivera. "There are courts and lawyers. There is a constitution. But the law does not stop the squadrons of death."

3

Agent Gallucci of the Federal Bureau of Investigation, impatiently drummed his fingers on the desktop. As David Holt detailed the information his firm had gathered on Colonel Quesada, Gallucci stared out of his office window at the smog-gray skyline of Los Angeles.

Holt took a folder from his briefcase. "Here are photocopies of the death threats against my clients. Photographs of the murdered child and administrative assistant. A photo of the men who followed Mr. Marquez in San Salvador. These are photos of the Salvadoran soldiers who arrived in Miami. My client identified this man as one of the murderers of Ricardo Marquez. Other sources identify—"

Swiveling his chair around, Agent Gallucci interrupted the attorney. "Why don't you take all this to the Salvadoran Embassy?"

"Because this concerns the murder of an American citizen—"

"Who got killed in El Salvador. We don't investigate what happens in other countries."

"There is reason to believe that Quesada ordered the murder of Marquez from Miami. The murderers are now in the United States—"

"Reason to believe? What does that mean?"

"Quesada is the commander of the death squad. Marquez attempted to interview him in Miami. The next month, when Marquez traveled to El Salvador to report on terrorism directed against the land-reform programs, he noticed men following him through the city. He photographed those men before evading them—or believing he evaded them. The next day, while he was waiting to speak with my client, he was murdered with machetes."

"The State Department says he got killed in combat, in a cross fire between the army and the Communists."

"The autopsy will disprove that—"

"What autopsy?"

"The newspaper has sent a doctor to examine the body."

"Until the State Department issues another statement, he died in combat. Occupational hazard for newspapermen creeping around in other people's wars. Maybe you ought to take all this over to OSHA office."

"May I quote you on that?"

"I tell you what, Mr. Holt. Why don't you bring your clients in. We'll talk about all this. I'll call down the hall to the INS. We'll have one of their officers stop by to discuss extending your clients' visas. Chances are all this will take months to sort through."

"That won't be possible."

The middle-aged FBI agent faked surprise. "You mean, your clients won't come in to talk about this? You implied you had their full cooperation—oh...I know what the problem is. They're illegal. You're representing some Commie wetbacks, aren't you? What do you intend to do, sell your crazy story to the networks?''

''My clients are in fear for their lives—''

''You better be in fear for your freedom, Mr. Pro Bono. And your practice. Aiding and abetting illegal entry into this country is a crime. You want to go to prison?''

Holt returned the documents and photos to his briefcase. He glanced at his watch. ''Do you watch the news programs in the evenings, Agent Gallucci?''

''Sure. Got to know what's happening in the world.''

''Watch tonight.''

The attorney left the federal office without another word.

4

Technicians held spotlights. Sound men crowded around David Holt with microphones as other technicians readied TV cameras. On the steps of the Wilshire Boulevard Federal Building in the Los Angeles suburb of Westwood, Holt waited as the network crews readied their equipment. Federal employees returning from their lunch hour glanced at the impromptu news conference. But they passed without commenting or questioning; they saw the media and demonstrations every day.

A camerawoman signaled the attorney. "Ready here, Mr. Holt."

"Anytime," another technician called out.

"Sir. Please give us a voice level before you begin your statement."

"Certainly. Thank you all for coming at such short notice. For those of you who may not know me, I am David Holt, of the law firm Holt, Lindsey and Stein. Usually our firm handles corporate law. However, we often take cases on a pro bono basis if we feel they represent a worthy public issue. Last week, a dear friend died in El Salvador. Do you have your levels now?"

"Go ahead...."

"Perfect."

"Last week, the Latin American correspondent for the *San Francisco Globe*, Ricardo Marquez, died in Sonsonate, El Salvador. The United States ambassador reported to the American public that Mr. Marquez died in a cross fire between government and rebel forces.

"That is a lie. Marquez was murdered by members of the *Ejercito de los Guerreros Blancos*, the Army of White Warriors, a death squad founded in December of 1979 to defeat the reforms of the Salvadoran government. I have a cable from San Salvador—"

Holt held up a telex. "We sent a pathologist to exhume and examine the body. The doctor reports that Marquez was hacked to death. He was beheaded and mutilated.

"We have witnesses to this crime.

"We have identified the murderers.

"The commander of this death squad lives in Miami Beach, Florida. At this moment, the Salvadorans responsible for the murder of Ricardo Marquez, an American citizen, enjoy the protection of the United States government.

"The Federal Bureau of Investigation threatened our witnesses with deportation to El Salvador, where they face certain death.

"Tomorrow, I will go to our nation's capitol to present this information to the United States Congress.

"This crime demands justice!"

5

A late afternoon breeze stirred the branches of the oak, the new leaves rustling with a sound like flowing water. The breeze lifted the helipad's Day-glo orange wind sock away from the pole, then swept across the fields beyond Stony Man Farm to sway the trees screening the installation from the highway.

His chest heaving, Carl Lyons sucked down cool air heavy with forest scents and the wet-earth smell of the roads and pathways still muddy from the spring rains. The cynical ex-cop, hardened and scarred by wars in the streets of Los Angeles, and more recently, in the secret dirty wars fought by Able Team, watched the wind caress the Virginia landscape. He saw Rosario Blancanales leave the farmhouse. In an easy jog, his Puerto Rican partner started across the hundreds of yards of pasture toward Lyons.

Lyons returned to his karate exercises. A heavy bag swung from one of the oak's lower branches. Four feet long, eighteen inches in diameter, the vinyl bag weighed a hundred pounds. To hit it approximated hitting a standing two-hundred-pound opponent. Lyons had raised the bottom of the bag to the level of his own crotch. The top twelve inches of the bag represented the opponent's head and face. In the hour of his workout, he had progressed through punches, elbow strikes, knee lifts, and right-leg front kicks. Now the left-leg kicks. . . .

He gave the bag a shove to get it swinging. In appropriate stance, he waited as the bag swung back, then snapped his left foot into the crotch zone. The second kick slammed the bag back an instant later. The third kick came as fast as Lyons could drive it into the rag-packed bag.

Kicking fast and hard, Lyons never let the bag swing forward. It hung at an angle as his kicks slammed the heavy bag back. After twenty-five kicks, he let his momentum carry him forward. He slammed his left elbow into the throat zone, stepped past the bag and whirled to drive his right fist into his imaginary opponent's kidney even as his left arm screamed with pain. Ignoring the pain, he wiped sweat from his eyes as Rosario Blancanales jogged up.

"Ready for a party?"

Lyons reached for his sweat shirt. "Mack sending us out again?"

"I'm serious. A party." Blancanales looked at the huge bruise on Lyons's left arm. A calm, quiet ex-Green Beret born in Puerto Rico, Blancanales served as medic, interpreter and indigenous-operations specialist for Able Team.

A week before, in the Sierra de Chucus of Guatemala, Lyons had assaulted a Huey troopship in an attempt to block the escape of the would-be Nazi dictator of Central America, Miguel de Unomundo. While Blancanales and Gadgets and a squad of Quiche Indians annihilated the last soldiers of Unomundo's army of Fascist mercenaries, Lyons dueled with the troop-ship's doorgunners—his full-auto twelve-gauge Atchisson against an M-60. Lyons killed one gunner, then another, but suffered a wound: as he took cover behind a burning truck, a burst from the dying gunner's weapon smashed through the door and windshield of the truck, a slug throwing the truck's rearview mirror into Lyons's arm.

"Why don't you take a break?" Blancanales said. "Let that heal before—"

"It's nothing," Lyons told him.

"Yeah? It's okay already?" Blancanales poked a fingertip into the wound. "How's that feel?"

Lyons recoiled, his left hand clawing with pain, his face going tight. He clenched his right fist. "Son of a bitch!"

"How's it feel when you're slamming it into that punching bag? You getting into pain? Macho masochism?"

Lyons grinned against the pain. "Nerve noise. Just nerves transmitting noise to my brain. Nothing real."

Blancanales cocked back his fist. "Ignore this one!"

Deflecting the fist with his shoulder, Lyons hooked a foot behind his partner's right foot, dropped him onto the grass. He went into a down-strike, as if to finish Blancanales with a fist to the temple. As the fist came down, Blancanales rolled to the side, scissored his legs around Lyons's legs, dropped him.

On his ass in the grass, Lyons laughed. "You know all the tricks. So what's this party you're talking about? April set us up with some of her friends? No thanks!"

"No, this is a Washington party. A reception."

"Politicians? Bureaucrats? Only if I can take my Atchisson. Do some rat killing."

"You're positively antisocial—"

"Nah, man. I just know who's bringing this country down."

"It's a reception for a retired Salvadoran general. He's merging his shipping company with an American multi-national corporation."

Lyons stopped his cynical jokes. Squatting now, he waited for more information.

"You remember the briefing on Unomundo?" Blancanales asked. Lyons nodded. "I read through this general's background file. There wasn't anything definite, but there are most definitely some questions as to how the general financed his operations. He also associates with a clique of colonels and landowners in self-exile from El Salvador. We could meet some very interesting people."

"Brognola assign this to us?" Lyons asked. Standing, he paced the pasture. The pasture's mud stained his sweat pants.

"It's not an assignment. Seems the Salvadorans invited a senator friend of Hal's. But the senator can't stomach these people, so he passed the invitations to Hal, and he passed them to me. He sent a set of Senate credentials with the tickets. We'll be the senator's personal aides. What do you say? It's free."

"Could be a mistake. If we ever go undercover on an Unomundo operation, one of the general's people could remember us from this reception."

"How could you ever go undercover in El Salvador?

They look at you, they know where you're from. You don't even speak the language.''

"All right, I'll chance it. I want to see what they look like. We take weapons?''

Blancanales laughed as he got to his feet. ''Hey, Carl. It's a party. Drinks. Food. Good times.''

"Sounds more like a recon to me.''

Blancanales nodded. ''That, too.''

6

Union musicians played instrumental renditions of Beatles songs. Near the bandstand in the hotel reception hall, couples danced. The women wore designer gowns and flashing jewelry, the men formal attire.

In rented tuxedos, Lyons and Blancanales stood at the bar. A hotel bartender in a white coat served drinks to the crowd of guests.

Annoyed by the starched collar of his formal shirt, Lyons twisted his head from side to side. He hooked a finger inside the collar and pulled. But the stiff collar and the bow tie did not stretch.

"Go dance with someone," Blancanales suggested. "A bit of sweat will make the collar softer."

"How do you say it in Spanish?"

"Don't try to fake it, you might say something weird. English is good enough."

"Most of these people are speaking French," Lyons commented.

"And Castilian," Blancanales added.

"Who are all the Europeans?" Lyons asked, looking at a tall blond woman in a sequined red gown. "I thought this was a Salvadoran party."

"Rich Salvadorans. They want us to think they're Europeans, but they're not."

The blond woman—lithe, perhaps twenty-five years old, her face a perfect oval of finely sculpted features touched with powder and rich red lipstick—laughed with a group of men. Two stocky men, one blond and balding, the other with crew-cut salt-and-pepper gray hair, spoke loud in English. The blond woman turned to her escort, whispered to him. The middle-aged Latin, his hair glistening with pomade, smiled. The blond saw Lyons watching her.

Her lips froze in midword as her eyes examined the stranger. The Latin man waited for her to complete her whispered confidence. Then he looked from her face to Lyons. The Latin scowled.

Lyons laughed at the middle-aged man's jealousy. A hand jerked Lyons aside.

"Be cool, Ironman," Blancanales hissed. "That's the general."

"Who's the beauty?"

"How should I know?" Blancanales pushed Lyons through the crowd. "One thing I do know, it's less than diplomatic to make eyes at the main man's girl friend."

At the buffet table, Lyons grabbed a handful of sliced roast beef. He took a plate and held it under his chin to catch the blood dripping from the rare-cooked beef.

"Pardon me for living," Lyons said with his mouth full of meat and blood. "I'm just an animal on the prowl."

Blancanales took a plate. A Latin waiter served him slices of beef and turkey. Blancanales held up a fork and spoke to Lyons.

"Now that you're moving in high society. . .this is a fork. Watch, I will demonstrate how to use it."

"You!" a Spanish-accented voice demanded. "Who are you?"

The Americans turned—Blancanales with a speared slab of white turkey meat in his mouth, Lyons holding a hunk of beef dripping blood—to see two young Latins confronting them.

Except for their expensive suits and gold wrist-watches, the Latins looked like soldiers. Their backs ramrod-straight, they wore their hair military-short. Their wide shoulders and barrel chests stretched the fabric of their expensive Italian suits. As the two members of Able Team studied the men who demanded their identities, one of the Salvadorans raised a hand to point at Lyons's chest.

"I said, who—"

Lyons grasped the young soldier's immaculate hand, shook it like a long-lost friend. He talked through a mouthful of beef. "I'm Mike! I'm pleased to meet you. Who are you?"

The Salvadoran tore his hand free. He grabbed a napkin from the caterer's table and wiped the smeared blood and gravy from his hand and shirt cuff. The elegant diplomats and women around them stared.

"You come with us. We are security."

Blancanales turned to Lyons. "See what happens when you flirt with a general's girl friend?"

"I didn't even talk to her."

"Come!" the other soldier demanded.

"Sure, where you want to go?" Lyons grinned. He reached toward the rows of wine bottles. He saw a waiter stripping a champagne bottle of its foil and wire. "Let me get a drink—"

As Lyons's hand closed around the neck of the unopened bottle, the first soldier seized Lyons's left arm, his fingers digging into the healing wound under the coat sleeve. Lyons's face went white with pain and a guttural roar rose in his throat as he reflexively smashed the soldier on the side of the head with the champagne bottle.

The cork shot across the room. An explosion of champagne foam sprayed Lyons and the onlookers. Stunned, the soldier dropped. Women shrieked as their escorts pulled them back from the violence. Men pushed through the crowd. Blancanales scanned the ballroom, saw the general and three other Salvadorans approaching.

Champagne ran off Lyons's rented tuxedo. The bottle in his hand dripped foam. He looked around him at the faces of the staring men and women. Lyons laughed, then drank from the foaming bottle.

The second soldier jerked a 9mm auto-pistol from his belt. Blancanales kicked him in the crotch, the force of the kick lifting the young man off the floor. The pistol flashed, a slug punching into the parquet floor.

In the screaming and panic, shoulder to shoulder with satins and diamonds and bow ties, Lyons and Blancanales ran for the door. A Salvadoran stood at the door, his eyes searching the crowd, his right hand under his coat.

As the two men of Able Team shoved through the elegant guests, the Salvadoran saw them. His right hand closed around a shoulder-holstered pistol, but the pistol never cleared his coat.

Lyons drove a full power front kick into the Salvadoran's solar plexus. In the crowding and confusion, the kick hit an instant late, just as the Salvadoran's forearm crossed his body.

Bones snapped. Screaming, the Salvadoran fell back, his auto-pistol clattering to the floor, lost among the feet of the guests rushing out the door. Smashing the champagne bottle down on the Salvadoran's head, Lyons followed Blancanales and the crowd into the hotel corridor.

They jogged into the lobby. Shoving through the plate-glass doors, they ran past the taxis and limousines lining the hotel's driveway. Their breath clouded in the cool spring night. Blancanales looked at Lyons, noting the champagne soaked tuxedo, the bits of glass sparkling on the sleeves and lapels. The Puerto Rican laughed, put his arm around his partner's shoulders as they ran.

"Lyons, you're my friend, but this is the last time I take you to a party."

7

Passengers bound for Washington, D.C., crowded from the lounge to board the jet. Floyd Jefferson ran to a pay phone. He punched the number of David Holt's Mill Valley home. After a few rings, he heard the voice of Mrs. Holt.

"Good morning."

"Good morning, ma'am. This is Floyd Jefferson. The plane's leaving and Mr. Holt isn't here yet. Did he—"

"He left an hour ago. Could there be a traffic problem?"

"I don't know....I'll call the office."

"And I'll call the office if he calls here."

"Goodbye, Mrs. Holt."

The young journalist punched another number. The law-office receptionist answered.

"Holt, Lindsey, and Stein...."

"This is Floyd Jefferson. I'm calling from the airport. Mr. Holt and I are supposed to fly east this morning, but he hasn't shown up. In fact, he just missed the plane. Did he call? Leave a message?"

"No, Mr. Jefferson, Mr. Holt hasn't called. Perhaps a jam delayed him. Why don't you give me your number? I'll call you when he calls."

He read the number to her. "It's a pay phone but I'll be here. I'll get seats on the next flight east and wait by the phone."

Four hours later, he called the office for the tenth time. He heard the alarm in the receptionist's voice before she told him.

"The police just called! They found Mr. Holt's car in Oakland."

Jefferson felt his body go cold. "What about him?"

"They don't know. There was no...no blood, no sign of a struggle in the car, they said, but...."

"I'll call back in an hour."

Jefferson ran to the ticket clerk, bought a ticket to San Diego.

8

On the sidewalk, girls jumped rope. Jefferson cruised past in his rented sedan, his eyes scanning the parked cars, the doorways, the three Hispanic men standing at the corner liquor store.

He watched behind him in the rearview mirror, then turned right. Continuing around the block, he glanced at every car. A panel truck appeared on the narrow street, the late afternoon sunlight flashing from its blue lacquer. The customized van eased into the narrow driveway of one of the small houses lining the barrio street. A teenager got out.

Jefferson continued his loop. Approaching the apartment house again, he parked and waited. The three men at the liquor store door went their separate ways, one man carrying his six-pack of beer to a truck loaded with a lawn mower and tools, the other two walking away. The four young girls jumping rope continued their game.

Finally, he left the car. He hurried to the entry of the Riveras' apartment house. At the stairs, he stopped and listened to the televisions and voices and footsteps in the old building. A woman laughed behind a door. Applause came from a TV. A toilet flushed. He climbed the stairs silently, easing his weight slowly on the old wood of each step.

He stayed against the hallway wall, sliding his feet along the old linoleum to avoid announcing his approach with footsteps. At the Riveras' door, he stood absolutely still, his back pressed against the wall, listening with his ears and with the flesh of his back.

Nothing moved inside the apartment. Jefferson took a quarter from his pocket and dropped it. The coin rang on the linoleum. It rolled to a stop against the door. Jefferson listened. He heard nothing beyond the door.

Without moving from against the wall, he knocked, rapping his knuckles against the wood three times, hard. The knocks sounded like shots in the quiet hallway. He heard no one inside the apartment.

He tried the knob. It turned. He eased the door open an inch, then shoved it open. Slamming against the wall, the door bounced half-closed. Jefferson eased one eye past the door frame.

Papers with children's writing covered the table. An overturned Styrofoam cup had spilled coffee on the windowsill. Jefferson pushed the door flat against the wall. He peered through the crack between it and the door frame to confirm that no one stood behind the door.

"Señor Rivera! Señora!"

He heard only the sound of cars passing on the street.

9

Weaving through the evening traffic, Jefferson watched the cars around him and behind him. His eyes on the rearview mirror, he almost rear-ended a truck. Brakes screeched as his old Volkswagen rattled to a stop only inches short of a crash. Jefferson felt his hands shaking as he waited for the signal to change.

After returning to San Francisco, he had called the Holt residence. A police officer answered the phone. The officer explained that the police had no reason to suspect kidnapping: David Holt could have simply parked his car and walked away to begin a new life, perhaps with a young woman. The police refused to consider any political or international intrigues until the investigators exhausted every other explanation. The officer suggested Jefferson call the Federal Bureau of Investigation.

Jefferson had other priorities. He did not want to disappear also. He would go "underground." However, he needed his bankbook, his .38 revolver and the negatives of his photos of the Salvadorans in Miami. He would chance a stop at his apartment.

Strolling couples and shoppers crowded the sidewalks of his neighborhood. He cruised past, his eyes searching the parked cars and sidewalks. The diversity of the people defeated his precautions. He saw Hispanics, blacks, Anglos, Orientals. Muscled young men with perfect hair and designer jeans window-shopped in groups. Hundreds of cars took every space at the curb. Other cars double-parked. A car full of Hispanic teenagers was parked in a driveway while the driver ran into a liquor store.

On his street, Jefferson saw a thousand shadows where they could hide.

A panel truck moved into a space two addresses down from his apartment complex; the driver—a young Chicano in a Windbreaker, slacks and Cuban heels—got out and saw that he had parked next to a fire hydrant. He restarted the truck and drove away. Jefferson swerved into the space. Tonight, a fifty-dollar parking ticket would be the least of his problems.

Leaving the driver-side door unlocked, he got out of the car. He did not go to his apartment. A friend's room overlooked the street and the entry to Jefferson's apartment complex. Jefferson ran up the wooden stairs to the second floor of the partitioned Victorian house.

"Who's that there?" a voice questioned when he knocked.

"Floyd."

"Ah...say, brother. Could you come back later?"

"I got a problem. I got a serious problem."

"This is an inconvenient time."

"I don't care who you're screwing! This is life and death—"

The door opened. Jefferson stepped into the dim interior of the one-room apartment. The air smelled of marijuana and sweat. His friend Peter stood naked behind the door.

His ratted blond natural hairstyle clouding around the bronze tan of his face and shoulders, Peter grinned like a demon. From the double mattress on the floor, two young men looked at Jefferson.

"Want to make it a foursome?" Peter asked him.

"Hey, man. I'm hetero. How many times I got to tell you that." Jefferson went to the window and looked across to his apartment entry.

"We won't tell your wife!" one of the young men quipped from the mattress.

Jefferson took the phone. He dialed his landlady. "Hi, Miss Curran, this is Floyd. No, no problem with the rent. Reason I called is some friends of mine might be waiting for me. Salvadorans. Short hair. Muscles. Look like soldiers."

"Oh...so macho," the other young man on the mattress sighed. "Introduce us."

"You saw them? They left? Oh, shit."

"I'd be disappointed, too," Peter laughed.

"No, ma'am. I'm sorry I said that. I think I'll be gone for a few days. Talk to you later." Jefferson broke the connection, then dialed another number.

"Hey, Prescott? Working late? Yeah, this is Floyd. We didn't go. I'll tell you why. I'm coming down to the office. The congressman's in town? I got a story for him. Stay till I get to you. There in half an hour."

Peter introduced his lovers. "Craig. Allan. This is Floyd Jefferson. He works for the *Globe* sometimes. What's this life-and-death problem?"

"You still got that riot shotgun?" Jefferson asked Peter.

"Sure do. Never know when the Moral Majority's going to go Ayatollah ape-shit."

"I'll buy it from you." Jefferson took out his traveler's checks. "How much? Two hundred? Two fifty?"

"What's going on?"

"Three hundred. You can buy a new one tomorrow."

Peter forced a laugh. "Are you serious?"

"And a hacksaw. And all the shells you got."

"Floyd, if you're in trouble, just take it. You don't have to pay me."

Still naked, but his smiles and jokes gone, Peter went to the closet. He took out an old blue-steel Smith & Wesson with an eighteen-inch barrel and a three-round magazine. Returning to the bed, he checked the safety, then handed it to Jefferson. "It's loaded and cocked. There's a round of Number Six in the chamber. Next three are double-ought. Forget the money, just take it."

"No, I don't want any shit coming down on you—you two guys are witnesses. I'm buying this shotgun. Three traveler's checks, three hundred dollars. What about the shells and the hacksaw? And a wood rasp and some electrical tape."

"Here's all the bullets I've got. The hacksaw's down in my tool box, in my car—"

"How about...." Jefferson filled his pockets with twelve-gauge shells, then crossed the room to a plastic basket of dirty clothes. Pulling an old pair of Peter's jeans from the laundry, he slipped the shotgun's barrel and magazine into one pant leg, the stock into the other leg. "This'll do it."

"What's going on, Floyd?" Peter asked again.

"You see David Holt on the news last night? Talking about Ricardo Marquez?"

"Yeah. He said there's some kind of cover-up—"

"He disappeared this morning. And now I got Salvadorans dropping by my apartment. See you three later. Have a good time."

Floyd Jefferson left them in stunned silence. Going down the stairs, he kept his eyes on the street. He looked down into the interiors of cars and trucks. He saw no one in the parked cars. No one loitered in the quiet shadows.

As he crossed the street, he slipped out his keys. If they hit him, it would be as he opened the security gate. The colored decorative lights tinting the modern stucco apartment house also illuminated the shrubbery. Jefferson saw no one near the entry. His right hand gripped the shotgun; the key was ready in his left. He jogged to the gate and opened it fast.

The courtyard glowed with soft green light from the pool. Jefferson paused to scan the walkways. He heard stereos and televisions. Someone closed a window.

Jefferson ran to his apartment. He unlocked the door and threw it open, but did not enter. His back to the wall, he listened for movement inside. Finally, he reached in and flicked the light switch.

They had ransacked the apartment. Every drawer had been emptied, every closet searched, every envelope of photos and negatives opened. Black-and-white prints, color prints, strips of negatives and contact sheets littered the floor. They had pulled the framed prints from the wall and torn off the backings in their search.

Now Jefferson searched the apartment. Leading with the shotgun, he checked the closets, the bedroom, the bathroom. He reached under the bookshelf where he kept his .38 pistol. Gone. He felt only the spring clips that had held it.

In the bathroom, his colognes and medicines and shampoos covered the floor. He saw the spilled box of Arm and Hammer baking soda. Reaching inside the box, he took out the plastic canister.

They had not found the negatives.

Searching through the litter on the floor, Jefferson picked up his bankbook. He didn't bother with clothes. He had enough for three days packed in a suitcase in his Volkswagen.

"Vacation time," he joked to himself, giving his looted apartment a last look. He turned off the light before he stepped out.

He avoided the front entry. Jogging to the rear of the courtyard, he stopped at the security gate to the parking spaces. He listened for a minute, then slowly, silently eased the steel gate open.

Shotgun ready, he crept around the rear of the building to the driveway. He walked quickly but stealthily to the street. Stopping at the end of the driveway, he peered around the corner.

A Salvadoran, his back to Jefferson, crouched beside the entry. In his dark jacket and dark slacks, he appeared to be only the shadow of a shrub. His close-cut black hair glistened red from the decorative spotlights.

On the street, a rented four-door Dodge idled, both curb-side doors open. Another Salvadoran waited behind the wheel. Jefferson strained to see any others, his eyes searching the shadows, the doorways, the cars parked at the curb. He saw only the two Salvadorans.

He waited. As his pulse raced, he forced himself to breathe slowly, to calm himself. He felt the stock of the shotgun become slick with his sweat.

Rising from his crouch, the Salvadoran at the entry looked into the apartment courtyard. He made a hand signal to the other man. Jefferson saw a rope in the man's hand.

They intended to take him alive, Jefferson realized. Maybe for the negatives. Maybe for interrogation.

If he could take one of them, maybe he could help Mr. Holt. Jefferson looked at the shrubs screening the apartments from the street. The Salvadoran waiting in the Dodge would not see him. But could he cross the flower beds silently? No.

The answer came to him. Forget the man at the entry. Take the Salvadoran waiting in the car. Put the shotgun up against his gut, tell him to drive to a police station. All right....

Easing from the corner, the shotgun clammy in his hands beneath its camouflage of pant leg, Jefferson took one slow step at a time. He watched the man at the entry. Shrubs blocked the view of the man in the car. Jefferson moved silently through the shadows and the soft colors of the decorative floodlights.

Headlights blinded him. A car lurched to a stop in the driveway. Squinting through the glare, Jefferson saw a form lean from the driver's window.

"Who are you? What're— Floyd? Is that you, Floyd?"

Disregarding his neighbor's questions, Jefferson ran to the idling Dodge. He jumped into the front seat, the Smith & Wesson riot shotgun pointed at the midsection of the Salvadoran. The Salvadoran jerked an auto-pistol from a shoulder holster.

From a distance of eighteen inches, Jefferson fired, the blast deafening him, the backsplash of blood hot on his face and hands. The Salvadoran groaned once and died as Jefferson scrambled backward, falling out of the car.

On his back on the street, he saw the second Salvadoran running at him, a pistol in his hand flashing. A slug zipped past the young journalist's face.

He tromboned the riot gun and pointed the torn, blood-slick pant leg covering the muzzle at the death-squad soldier rushing him.

A blast of double-ought slammed the Salvadoran back. Shattered glass fell to the entry's walkway as Jefferson scrambled to his feet. Lights came on everywhere on the block. Jefferson ran to his car and jerked the door open.

His shaking, bloody hands dropped the keys twice before he jammed the key into the ignition. Redlining the Volkswagen's old engine, Jefferson roared away in first gear.

Wiping blood and shreds of flesh from his face and hands, Jefferson drove to the civic center. His friend

Bob Prescott worked for U.S. Congressman Buckley as a legal researcher. The congressman had a reputation for investigating conspiracies and federal intrigues.

In front of the congressman's district office, Jefferson looked at the other parked cars and trucks before turning off his old Volkswagen's engine. Working the shotgun's action to chamber another shell, he set the safety. He wrapped the pant legs around the muzzle and stock again. Acting as naturally as his nerves allowed, he left the car, his eyes always moving, searching every shadow. He opened the hood and found a hacksaw and a roll of tape in his tool kit. He took his overnight case.

Often, Jefferson knew, Congressman Buckley— through Floyd's friend Prescott—had tipped Ricardo Marquez to impending scandals and indictments. And in the past year, the congressman had become a leading critic of the Administration's blunderings in Central America. Now Floyd Jefferson had a story for Buckley.

As he went up the steps to the office, a car squealed around the corner. Inside the plate-glass doors, Jefferson paused to watch the car. It skidded to a stop.

His gut twisted as the driver's door flew open, the interior light revealing two Hispanics in the car.

Clutching the shotgun, Jefferson ran upstairs to the sanctuary of the congressman's office.

10

Hal Brognola ignored the ringing telephone. Turning in the bed, he pulled a pillow over his head. He knew it would not be an important call. The White House or Stony Man would only call via the secure line. His pager would then sound an electronic tone. The ringing stopped as the answering machine in his study clicked on.

An amplified voice broke the silence of the house: "Hal? Hal Brognola? This is Congressman Buckley. I'm calling from San Francisco. I have a problem I need to discuss—"

Brognola groped for the phone. "Chris Buckley?" he whispered, to avoid waking up his wife. "Ah...this is Hal. What's the problem?"

"Sorry to wake you up. But I've got a bad situation and I need help with it tonight."

"Well, the Justice Department doesn't operate like that. Litigation can take years. Have you called—"

"The police? The FBI? The FBI may be involved in this problem. But on the other side. I thought you could put me in touch with some...specialists."

"Don't know what you mean, Mr. Buckley."

"Is this a secure line?"

"No."

"Give me the number. I'll call on the other—"

"Mr. Buckley, *if* I had a secure line, and *if* I could somehow help you with this problem you have, it would be a matter of authorization. And that authorization would be available only after consultation with my bureau. We have regulations and procedures."

"Remember *Las Islas de Sabana*?"

"What did you say?"

"Let's talk on the secure line."

Brognola gave him the number.

11

Floyd Jefferson watched the boulevard. Three floors below the congressman's office, a light came on in the rented Dodge. A Salvadoran left the car. Jefferson watched the man run to a pay phone down the block.

In the inner office, Congressman Buckley finally hung up the phone. The door opened, a swath of light silhouetting Jefferson against the window before he could jump to the side.

"Sir! Turn off that light. They're down there."

"Oh...yes. I'll—" Buckley returned to his office for an instant. The suite of offices went dark again.

Below, the Salvadoran glanced up to the office windows as he talked on the pay phone.

"They haven't left?" The middle-aged, balding congressman joined Jefferson at the window.

"It's called surveillance. They're just down there watching. One's still in the car, the other one's calling his boss, I bet."

"Has Bob seen anything?" Buckley asked. His aide, Bob Prescott, stood guard in the lobby. If the Salvadoran attempted to enter the building, he would warn Buckley and Jefferson.

"Checked with him a minute ago. Nothing. What did they say in Washington?"

"He told me to wait. He'll need to make a few calls."

"Who did you call?"

"It would be a violation of the President's confidence if I told you the man's name—"

"I meant, was it the FBI? Mr. Holt went to the FBI office down in Los Angeles yesterday. He told them what he knew. And now he's gone."

"No, it wasn't the bureau. This group is independent. That's all I can tell you."

"Did you tell them about the two goons I shot?"

Buckley nodded. He glanced past Jefferson to the boulevard. The Salvadoran at the pay phone hung up the receiver, then punched another number. The middle-aged congressman ran his hand over his balding head. He turned to the young reporter.

"You realize the story you told me, this...intrigue—does not mitigate the fact that you shot two men. I have no doubt the police are now searching for you. I advise you to consult a criminal attorney very, very soon."

"Hey, man. You're a lawyer, you been a lawyer all your life—"

"Twenty-five years."

"You run around in Washington Dee of Cee, talking laws, writing laws, voting on laws," fumed Jefferson, "but just because there are police and courthouses and jails doesn't mean the law is real. You grow up like I did, you'll know there's laws and then there are people. There are people who won't cross the street in the middle of the block and then there are people who don't give a shit if it's your body they serve for Sunday dinner. And in this particular instance, we are dealing with some people of the latter variety. So, you'll forgive me if I don't give the police a whole lot of thought. If I live through all this, then I'll go talk with the police. Because those goons down there, those Salvadorans, they come from a different world.''

"Floyd...." The congressman walked through the darkness of his office as he considered his response to what the young man had declared. "Do you actually believe I am a stranger to reality? As you say, there are laws and there are people. I am not unfamiliar with conflicts between the law and reality. Yet I serve and obey the law.''

"But you just called some dudes on the phone who aren't legal, right? If they're not police and they're not FBI, then chances are—''

"Let me qualify what I said. I serve and obey the law whenever possible.''

"Uh-huh. I get it. You made an exception in this case. Does that exception have anything to do with the reality that some goons are parked in front of your office? They didn't know I was coming here. They didn't even recognize me. They were watching you. Is that why you made an exception?''

Inside the inner office, the phone rang. Buckley rushed away without answering Jefferson. The young reporter heard the door lock before the ringing stopped. As the murmuring, almost inaudible voice of the congressman came through the thick oak panels of the office door, Jefferson took the old Smith & Wesson from the floor.

Surrounded by walls of law volumes—the leather-bound two-hundred-year history of the world's most successful experiment in justice—Floyd Jefferson put the hacksaw to the shotgun and, as fast as he was able, sawed off the barrel to fourteen inches.

12

In the predawn darkness, a chill wind swept from the Smoky Mountains. Able Team gathered at the Stony Man Farm helipad. Hal Brognola had called from Washington only half an hour before. Now the three men of Able Team waited. Unshaved, their close-cut hair windblown, their sport coats and slacks pulled from hangers, they waited for the helicopter that would take them to Dulles International. Lyons knotted his tie, Blancanales smoothed the wrinkles from his slacks, Gadgets listened to an early-morning talk show on a pocket stereo.

They had not needed to pack their suitcases. Cases packed with clothing and equipment stood ready at all times. They needed only to know their destination, then take the proper prepacked case of clothing and equipment. Professionals, they knew action might come at any time.

"I didn't really get what Hal told me," Lyons wondered aloud. "What do you think's going on? He said, 'Until we consult with the bureau, you three have highest authority.' Does that mean we hit the problem first, then the federals take over? I was still half-asleep, or I would have quizzed him on that one—"

"Sounds like we're in the gray zone on this," Gadgets answered him.

"Sounds like we're walking point for the FBI," Blancanales said.

"No." Gadgets shook his head. He wound up his transistor radio's earphone wire. "I asked Hal if we would have access to bureau equipment in San Francisco. And he said—" Gadgets pressed a button on the miniature stereo. Hal Brognola's voice came from the tiny speaker: "Absolutely not. Under no circumstances will you identify yourselves to law enforcement personnel of any other agency, local or federal. There are several uncertainties that must be resolved before we can request liaison or technical services...."

Gadgets clicked off the replay. *"Comprende* dat jivo?"

"You record everything?" Lyons asked.

"When I get a call from Washington, and the man's talking jive, I record it. It was recordings that got Tricky Dick in the shit. I'm hoping recordings might keep this Wizard clean."

Blancanales shook his head. "Hal wouldn't send us out without authorization."

"He never sent us out with conditional authorization before," Lyons countered.

"Conditional highest authority," Gadgets laughed. "I mean, that's jive."

Rotor throb came from the east. Their heads turned simultaneously to the sound. Lyons laughed cynically. "How about Conditionally Beyond Sanction? Conditionally Beyond the Law? No way. Mack Bolan acts beyond conditions, and so do we. Sometimes, my friends, the law's got nothing to do with it, and that's one condition I can understand."

13

In the oily scum of a tidal flat in San Francisco Bay, a dog discovered a bundle wrapped in black plastic. The dog sniffed at a rip in the plastic bag. A man in a sweat suit and Windbreaker whistled, once, twice.

The man squinted through the gray dawn light. As he waited on the beach, he saw his dog tear at the glistening black object. Something gray appeared.

Backing away, the dog barked. It barked incessantly, circling the gray and black bundle. Impatient with the dog's exploring, the man whistled again before jogging away. He looked back and saw that his dog did not follow him.

"Aqui! Venga aquí perro loco!"

But the dog continued barking. Cursing in three languages, the dog's owner picked up a stick. He found a path through the muddy flotsam and driftwood of the tidal flat. Waving the stick, he shouted at the dog. *"Vengase, perro!"*

The dog left the bundle. Splashing through shallow mud, the dog ran to its master and barked. Then it returned to the bundle, circling it and barking.

Dirtying his expensive jogging shoes, the man pursued the dog. He splashed past the bundle and swung the stick at the dog's hindquarters. Dodging away, the dog tore at the plastic of the bundle again.

An arm fell out. Gray against the black muck, the arm seemed to glow in the half-light.

Not believing what he saw, the jogger stepped closer. He saw the form of a torso inside the plastic. The arm, with the slight muscles of a man who had always worked in an office, showed the rust brown stains of crusted blood.

Flame had curled and blackened the fingers. Like a claw, the scorched hand reached mud.

As Able Team arrived at the office of United States Congressman Chris Buckley in the metropolitan center of the city, the San Francisco police and the men from the office of the coroner removed the mutilated corpse of David Holt from the mud flats of the bay.

14

Able Team cruised through the early-morning quiet of the San Francisco Civic Center. Though the light of dawn flashed from the plate-glass walls of the high-rise towers, darkness still held the streets and boulevards. Neon lights blinked. The blue white points of mercury arc streetlights seared the gray air.

Arriving by commercial transcontinental jet at the international airport, the team had rented two new Ford sedans. Gadgets drove alone in one, Lyons chauffeured Blancanales in the other. Because they would work without liaison or backup, they carried all their gear with them—weapons, radios, clean clothes, even two shopping bags full of canned drinks and food.

Only an hour after their landing, they followed the freeways to the end of the peninsula and the district offices of Congressman Chris Buckley.

They drove past the building without slowing. Lyons scanned his side of the boulevard, his eyes searching for anything extraordinary. Blancanales memorized every detail on the other side. In the seconds of their passing, they saw only an empty Volkswagen in a No Parking zone in front of the offices; a Dodge sedan parked in a Passenger Loading zone across the street, occupied by a Hispanic reading a newspaper; a truck driver wheeling a rack of bread into a restaurant. A street sweeper weaved along the boulevard, swinging wide around the illegally parked cars and delivery trucks, swerving to the curb to scour the gutters of filth and litter. Another Hispanic, his hands in the pockets of his suit, stood at the end of the block.

"No action on my side of the street," Lyons commented. "You see anything?"

"Tal vez sí, tal vez no," Blancanales answered. The Puerto Rican ex-Green Beret leaned low in the seat as he keyed his hand-radio: "Wizard, *que pasa?*"

"Nada."

"You see the one at the corner?"

"Latin American? About five-ten, strong?"

"That's him."

"Looked like the one in the car. Same build, same hair, same style coat."

"A flashy dresser," Blancanales added. "But the one in the car looked like he'd sat in those clothes all night."

"Oh yeah...."

Lyons heard the conversation through the earphone he wore. He needed no instructions from his partners. With the familiarity and routine learned in Able Team's dirty wars, he accelerated through the streets. After several smooth turns, he slowed and then parked on a street intersecting the boulevard. They now viewed the Dodge from the rear. The second Hispanic had gone to the parked Dodge. They saw the driver glance across the boulevard to the upper floors of the office building.

Gadgets drove past in his rented Ford. He crossed the boulevard and parked where he had an angle on the front of the congressman's office entry. He buzzed his partners on their radios.

"There's someone on the third floor," Gadgets told them, "looking down at the street."

"Seems the two in the car are surveillance," Blancanales answered.

Lyons joined the conversation. "Unless maybe they've waited all night for the office to open...or for someone to come out."

Able Team did not fear the interception of their radio transmissions. They used hand-radios designed and manufactured to National Security Agency specifications. Encoding circuits scrambled every transmission. Any technician scanning the bands would intercept only bursts of electronic noise.

Blancanales turned to Lyons. "We go in through the parking lot entrance?"

"They could have a car down there." Lyons looked to the daylight blazing from the glass of the towering buildings. "I say no meeting here. There'd be people coming to work while we talked. Much too public."

"Affirmative," Blancanales agreed as he opened the passenger door. He stepped out to the chill, damp morning. "Pay phone time."

As Bob Prescott talked on the phone, Jefferson observed the Salvadorans on the boulevard watching the office entry. Hearing what the congressman's aide proposed, Jefferson whipped around.

"They what?"

Prescott put his hand over the phone's mouthpiece. "He says they won't come in. Says it would compromise them. He wants us to go somewhere else where we can talk. So why don't we go over to my place on the hill? It's quiet and private."

"Forget that!"

"We could slip out the parking entrance. That way they—" Prescott nodded toward the boulevard "—wouldn't see us leaving."

"And what about the spooks?" Jefferson demanded. "They come in here, we've got a chance to check them out. We go where they want, we don't know what we're walking into."

"Floyd...." The congressman spoke with his sonorous media voice, his tone paternal and wise. "Though I don't always see eye to eye with the man I called, I trust him completely. I have no doubt he dispatched...ah, specialists...who are also trustworthy."

"Uh-huh. You trust them with your life. Hear this. Point number one, when Señor Rivera saw Ricardo Marquez get chopped up, he called the American Embassy. The next day, the *Blancos* came to kill him. They chopped up his son. Point number two, even after the embassy knew the *Blancos* had murdered an American citizen, they let those goons into the U.S. of A. Point number three, Mr. Holt went to the Federal Bureau of Investigation and told them he had a case against that Colonel Quesada and his gang of *macheteros*. The FBI told him to forget it. He didn't. He went public. He disappeared. Now you're telling me to trust some new people? No chance. You trust them with *your* life, not with mine."

The veteran politician considered Jefferson's words. He took the phone from his aide.

"Hello? This is Christopher Buckley. Who am I speaking to? Rosario? Rosario, I'm sorry to question your identity, but this is a very tense situation. Please give me the name of your commander.... Good. What did he tell you about our problem? Yes, yes, I'm aware the phones are insecure. But you do have some idea of the threat that confronts us. I'm attempting to negotiate a meeting, but...quite frankly, my young friend is afraid. And he has reason to be. We need to satisfy not only your need for security, but his also."

Buckley listened. "Yes, very good. I'm giving the phone to Floyd. Explain to him what you propose...."

Floyd Jefferson took the telephone. "Yeah?"

He heard a deep voice. "I'm Rosario. We can't come in with those—"

"Yeah, yeah. Listen, we can work out a place to meet, okay. But hear me, you don't know where it is until we get there. I'm not walking into any surprises...."

"No problem. I understand."

"You'll follow us—" Jefferson put his hand over the phone. "Mr. Buckley, you still have that black Lincoln, right?"

Buckley nodded. Jefferson spoke into the phone again. "A black Lincoln Continental. Easy to follow. You can't lose us. You let us go in, wait a minute or so, then you show up. But no surprises, see? I am one very jumpy dude lately, and if you try anything tricky, I just don't know what I'll do. Hear me?''

"I hear you. No surprises."

"All right. Give us ten minutes and we'll be coming out of the garage exit."

"See you soon."

"Yeah, later."

Hanging up the phone, Jefferson turned to the others. "We'll go to your place, Bob. They'll follow us. But man, this could be a setup."

Jefferson gripped the sawed-off Smith & Wesson riot gun. He had hacksawed the barrel off at fourteen inches, then cut off the stock to leave only a curled pistol grip. Black electrician's tape wrapped the grip. He held his finger straight against the safety and trigger assembly as he slapped the weapon's pump grip into the palm of his left hand.

"They make a move on us, they are gonna suffer...."

WATCHING IN THE REARVIEW MIRROR, Lyons saw the black Continental leave the office building's underground garage. The luxury car accelerated past. Putting his car into gear, Lyons entered the traffic of early-morning commuters and trucks. Blancanales, his passenger, cued Gadgets.

"That's the congressman's car."

Lyons spoke into his radio. "Let us lead. You stay out of sight. No reason to show them all our cards...."

"Check," Gadgets acknowledged.

Blancanales glanced at their partner as they passed.

Lyons stayed half a block behind the Lincoln as the black car sped from the Civic Center. In its back window, Lyons saw the silhouette of a head as someone looked back.

"Give them distance," Blancanales cautioned. "The kid sounded like a panic case."

"He's got reason." Lyons followed the Lincoln through a sweeping left-hand turn onto a one-way boulevard. "Most people couldn't cope with life on a death list."

"Remember Morales and Merida in our Guatemala hit?" Blancanales asked.

"They went to the wall. Guatemalans don't like traitors."

"Sharp dressers, remember? Italian silk suits, gold rings and watches."

"Merida looked more like a gigolo than a colonel."

"Remember the general's bodyguards the other night? At the reception?"

"So? You work for a rich general, you can afford flashy clothes."

"The ones in that parked Dodge—"

"I didn't see them."

"Men on a surveillance detail usually can't afford five-hundred-dollar suits—"

"I never could...."

"And if one can afford a five-hundred-dollar suit, he wouldn't wear it to sit in a parked car all night. Unless perhaps he worked for a billionaire."

Lyons laughed. "Hey, Rosario. I'm the paranoid. Not you. And what you're talking about is totally paranoid." Both knew Blancanales referred to a dangerously crazed billionaire known only too well to Able Team. "Why would Unomundo put a U.S. Congressman under surveillance?"

"Who hit his Azatlan base?"

"He doesn't know that we—"

"He saw you and Nate. Saw you face to face."

The Lincoln turned from the boulevard onto a winding avenue leading in to the homes on the Twin Peaks. Lyons slowed as a van roared past on the narrow avenue. He glanced at the van's passenger window and saw a middle-aged, gray-haired man in a conservative sport coat.

"Crazy San Francisco," Lyons commented. "Businessmen drive like hot-rodders. Pol, I want Unomundo, you know that. I got that Nazi's name on my list. But I'll have to go south to find him. He wouldn't send his people north."

"He sent his people to Texas...."

Lyons looked at Blancanales. "Yeah...but why this congressman? Buckley's a liberal, a dove. Peace to the world. He wrote that antigun amendment. Want to repeal the second amendment to the constitution. He thinks everyone should talk Russian—"

A buzz from their hand-radios interrupted Lyons. Blancanales keyed his radio

"What goes?"

"You see those two straights in the van?" Gadgets asked.

Blancanales looked ahead. He saw the white van tailgating the Lincoln. "Yeah, they're ahead of us. Behind the Lincoln."

"That's because they're following the Lincoln—"

Lyons keyed his radio. "When did you spot them?"

"About a mile back. The one on the passenger side has a walkie-talkie—"

"But I saw him. He's an Anglo. Holy shit! They're hitting Buckley—"

A hundred yards ahead, beneath the overspreading branches that shaded the street, the Lincoln had stopped at an intersection. A gray-haired, overweight Anglo in slacks and a sport coat ran from the van. Acceleration slammed the passenger-side door closed as the van swerved past the Lincoln and into the intersection. Then it came to a screeching stop in front of the Lincoln.

The gray-haired Anglo pulled an auto-pistol from a shoulder holster. Pointing the weapon with both hands, he advanced on the trapped Lincoln. The other man left the van and pointed a CAR-15 at the Lincoln's windshield.

Jerking back the Ford's transmission lever into first, Lyons stood on the accelerator. He saw the scene float past as if in slow motion.

The Anglo on the sidewalk looked toward the sound of the accelerating Ford. A blast came from the right rear window of the Lincoln, the Anglo gunman's face and head disintegrating in a spray of blood and flesh, the corpse flying backward. Even as Lyons's Ford whipped around the Lincoln, the Lincoln accelerated in reverse, tires smoking. The cars passed in opposite directions, only inches apart as the second gunman's Colt rifle sprayed a burst of 5.56mm slugs.

Lyons did not slow as slugs ricocheted off the Lincoln to hit the Ford, breaking the side window. Blancanales braced his Beretta 93-R in both hands. The silenced selective-fire pistol sent a three-round burst into the chest of the gunman, then the van blocked his line of fire.

As the Ford smoked through the intersection, Blancanales leaned from the window to sight on the gunman behind them. The wounded man staggered back, the Colt assault rifle still gripped in his right hand, his left hand clutching at his chest.

Pivoting in the seat to point the Beretta, Blancanales aimed another burst, but the slugs went into the sky as Lyons slammed on the brakes. A car backing from a driveway blocked the street. A housewife with three children in the back seat of her station wagon stared at the firefight.

In the rearview mirror, Lyons saw the wounded gunman lean against the van. One hand clutching his bloody chest, the gunman struggled to raise his assault rifle. Lyons slammed the Ford into reverse.

Tires smoking, the Ford roared backward through the intersection. Lyons screamed to his partner, "Down!"

The rear window exploded in fragments of sparkling glass. Slugs punched into the seats, slugs spiderwebbed the tempered glass of the windshield. Then the rapidly reversing Ford's rear bumper hit the gunman and the van.

Crushing both his legs, melding his body into the sheet metal and frame of the van, the crash killed the gunman instantly. The impact threw the van aside. Whipping wildly from side to side on the street, sideswiping a parked car, the Ford careered on. Lyons pumped the brakes, struggling to bring the car to a stop as it hurtled toward the Lincoln.

Skidding broadside in the street, the mangled Ford stopped. Lyons looked out the window to see the muzzle of a shotgun aimed at his face. The shotgun withdrew and the window of the Lincoln rolled down. A young man of indeterminate race—his face the color of mahogany—shouted out the window.

"Straight up the hill! We'll pass you—"

Lyons threw the shift into drive to accelerate past the smashed van. The Lincoln, then Gadgets's Ford followed a second later. After two blocks, Lyons pulled over to the side and let the Lincoln take the lead.

Looking over to his partner, Lyons saw Blancanales holding the Beretta beneath the window with one hand while he brushed broken glass out of his hair with the other. When the Lincoln and the second Ford sped past, Lyons followed.

Blancanales surveyed the interior of the rented car, the shattered windshield, the smashed rear windows, the twisted trunk. He looked down at the upholstery. A slug had punched through the seat, a protruding tangle of foam and vinyl indicating what the slug would have done to his gut. The Puerto Rican veteran of twenty years of war closed his eyes and shook his head. "I'm getting too old for this."

Speeding another five blocks through the narrow, winding streets, Lyons saw the Lincoln ease through the gate of a house screened from view by a wall overgrown with ivy. Gadgets's Ford followed. A few seconds later, Lyons parked his Ford on a brick driveway.

As Able Team got out of their cars, the dark young man—his sawed-off shotgun in one hand—ran to the gate and pushed it closed. Wood slats and interwoven ivy provided privacy from neighbors. The young man ran back to Able Team. With the wide eyes and manic grin of adrenaline, he shook hands with Lyons, Blancanales and Gadgets.

"I don't know who you guys are, but you are my friends forever."

15

Pacing through the black-and-white decor of the room, Jefferson told Able Team his account of the preceding three days. Though he had heard the story before, Congressman Buckley listened to it again as his aide, Bob Prescott, tape recorded Jefferson's words and took notes.

Able Team absorbed the story without comment, Blancanales also taking notes, Gadgets taping Jefferson's monologue on his pocket recorder. Lyons studied the interior of the aide's home.

Decorated with the stark design of Northern European high-tech, the room seemed to be a showroom of "minimalist chic": white vinyl couches, black plastic coffee table, gray industrial carpet over a floor finished in white plastic. Slender white enamel lamps focused light on African masks carved of ebony. On one wall, Lyons saw framed awards and photographs of Prescott with politicians and community leaders. One award commended the aide for work with the American Civil Liberties Union. But though his eyes wandered, Lyons did not miss a word Jefferson said.

The exhilaration and bravado of the street firefight faded from the young reporter's voice as he spoke. Panic returned as he described his meeting with the

Riveras and their children, the disappearance of David Holt, then the attempt to kidnap him.

"They took Mr. Holt, they took those people from El Salvador, and they tried to take me. I don't know what I'm on to, but they sure want to get me off it. You saw. Right there on the street, pistols and machine guns. They want me."

"To be exact," Congressman Buckley interrupted, "they want the photos. Those photos could establish an international conspiracy—"

"Linking Quesada to the murder of the reporter?"

Buckley explained. "The newspaper has photos Ricardo Marquez took of the men following him in San Salvador. Floyd has photos of Salvadorans—soldiers, he believes—meeting Colonel Quesada in Miami. And now the police have four dead men. If the men photographed in San Salvador went to Miami and then came here, the photos establish there is in fact a conspiracy. Of course, Quesada is implicated."

Blancanales shook his head. "Only indirectly."

"Any lawyer with a loud mouth," Lyons added, "could beat that charge. 'Constitutional right to free association, blah, blah, blah.'"

"Sir!" the congressman protested. "I am an attorney, I have been an attorney for twenty-five years, and I assure you the practice of law requires more than a loud mouth."

"Oh, yeah. Right. A lawyer needs a typewriter and a Cadillac, then he's all set."

"If you continue to disparage my profession," Buckley warned, "you can expect a discussion of the morality of *your* profession."

"Sure, let's talk about it." Lyons looked to Prescott. "You an attorney, too?"

The congressman's aide nodded.

"I notice you got six-foot walls, the legal limit. And a security system. And that sign for the private patrol. When you work for the ACLU, do you ever think about the people who can't afford to wall themselves off from the scum you set free?"

Gadgets laughed. He kicked Lyons in the shin. "Be cool. They're on our side."

"Not my side."

Speaking through a sneer, Buckley asked Lyons, "Tell me, Mr. Specialist. What are the qualifications to join a death squad? Perhaps you can help us understand these Salvadorans we confront. Did they find you in a prison? Or a metal institution?"

"Yeah, that's it. I'm a psychopath. I think children should have the freedom to walk to school. I think old people should have the freedom to leave their windows open. A society without fear. I got these totally crazy ideas in my—"

Blancanales interrupted Lyons. "Will you stop? We have a mission to complete. If you disagree with Mr. Buckley's politics, write him a letter. Floyd, those two men in the van weren't Salvadorans. You have any idea who they were, or how they may have come into this?"

"Yeah...maybe. When I was out in front of Quesada's place, when the Miami police put me down on the sidewalk, I looked over and I saw two who weren't Hispanics. One was blond and had fair skin showing through his hair on top. The other one had black hair speckled with gray. Both were heavies, big shoulders, thick necks.''

"But not the two who died today?"

Jefferson shook his head. "Never saw those two before."

"Never see them again, either." Lyons laughed.

Jefferson laughed with him. "Would've been in real trouble if you guys weren't behind us. Bob there—" Jefferson grinned to his friend "—he sees that machine gun pointed at his face and he freezes. I go ka-boom with my shorty and everything happens at once. Mr. Buckley hits the gearshift and Bob finally gets with it."

"Sorry," Prescott apologized. "My law school didn't teach counterterrorist tactics."

The telephone rang. Prescott left the living room.

Blancanales glanced at his notes, then asked Jefferson. "Did you recognize the two Salvadorans who came to your apartment house? Were they in the group you photographed in Miami?"

"I don't really know. It was dark and I was afraid and nervous and I didn't really look at their faces. It just happened too fast."

"Oh, my God!" Prescott gasped in the other room.

Jefferson turned. He opened his mouth to call out to Prescott. Lyons grabbed his arm to silence him. In a whisper, he warned the young man. "Police are looking for you, right? If that's a detective on the phone, he's listening for background voices."

"Oh, yeah, right."

They waited in silence as Prescott spoke. "Has Mr. Buckley been notified? No, he's not with me. Floyd

Jefferson? Yes, I know him. How could he be involved with that? Oh, of course. Thank you, officer. This is terrible. Thank you, of course I'll call if.... Goodbye.''

He returned to the others, his face blank with shock. ''The police found David Holt's body. He was tortured and murdered and then dumped in the bay.''

Congressman Buckley groaned. Jefferson started to speak, his mouth moved, but no sound came out. Lyons spoke first.

''Now we know they're serious.''

''It could've been me!'' Jefferson blurted out.

''But it wasn't,'' Blancanales told him.

''And it won't be,'' Lyons added. He looked to his partners. ''We got a plan yet?''

Jefferson's voice cracked with a sob. ''And—and that's what they did to the Riveras. Those little kids....''

''We don't know that,'' Blancanales told him.

''But they disappeared. I went there and it was like they were never there.''

''Think about it,'' Lyons told him. ''Gunmen show up to take the family. Two, three, maybe four of the *Blancos*. The mother and father know what's about to happen to them and their children. They'd fight. Kids would scream and cry. In a crowded apartment house? This isn't El Salvador—''

Jefferson nodded. ''People in the barrio watch out for each other.''

Lyons continued. ''Did they leave any clothes? Any luggage? A death squad wouldn't stop to pack up the family's belongings. Not with crying children and screaming neighbors and every homeboy on the street putting out rounds. This isn't El Salvador. Everybody's got a pistol or a shotgun. That death squad wouldn't make it to the street. I hope our esteemed representative—" Lyons turned to the mourning congressman "—will consider that fact the next time he authors an amendment to the constitution to repeal the right to bear arms. Those revolutionaries who wrote the constitution and bill of rights, they knew something you don't, Mr. Buckley."

"Stop it!" Blancanales lunged across the coffee table to silence Lyons.

"Yeah, yeah. I'll write a letter. I'll write a letter saying that a Mr. David Holt would be alive if he'd had a pistol in his pocket."

"I apologize for my loudmouthed associate," Blancanales told Buckley. "This is not the time for his speeches. He is a good man but he has no grace—"

"I got no grace," Lyons interrupted, "but I got the plan! There are three things we have to do. Protect Floyd Jefferson. Find and protect the Riveras. And break the *Guerreros Blancos*. We can't do that in San Francisco. I say we go to San Diego. Take Floyd with us."

"The police are looking for him," Gadgets countered. "They'll be watching the bus stations and the airport. We take him to the airport, he's gone. And not to San Diego."

Lyons shrugged. "We drive, then. Four hundred, five hundred miles. We dump that wrecked Ford, rent another one. We'll be there tonight."

"Take my motor home," Prescott offered. "If anyone got your license number today, all of you are fugitives. The police can trace you through those rented cars. They could intercept you on the highway."

"A motor home." Gadgets grinned. "What a luxury."

"Doesn't go very fast but it's very comfortable. Allow me to make one suggestion."

"What's that?" Lyons asked.

"Floyd, those photos from Miami. You should leave the negatives with our office—"

"No way!"

"For safekeeping. You lose the negatives, it all comes apart. We have no case to present to a court."

"No way, Bob." Jefferson shook his head, repeated, "No way. I got three killings to explain. That short little fella—" the young reporter pointed to the sawed-off shotgun near his feet "—will keep me alive. The negatives will keep me out of San Quentin. They go where I go."

Prescott shrugged. "If that's the way you want it. I'll go get my camper out of the garage."

The others sat in silence for a minute. They heard Prescott slide open garage doors. An engine started, sputtered, finally idled. Prescott's footsteps crossed the driveway. Looking to Lyons, Chris Buckley broke the silence with his first words since he had learned of the death of his friend.

"Perhaps I am a utopian. I believed I was acting in the best interests of the people of the United States when I proposed the amendment to limit the possession of weapons to security personnel. Until all this began, I did not doubt my reasoning that this is no longer a frontier nation, that this is now a nation governed by laws and protected by sworn personnel. I have faith in our country's criminal justice system—despite all its flaws—and I will always believe that law and justice and compassion, rather than force, will create an American culture that will be the envy of all nations.

"David Holt shared my beliefs. And now he is gone. You need not write that letter to me. Perhaps I should temper my utopian hopes with pragmatism. Perhaps we *are* still a frontier nation. It is one thing to hear of the suffering of others, it is another thing entirely to lose a friend. He was a fine man. Wealthy, yet concerned for those less fortunate. Totally committed to the future of our country. I have one request to make of you—"

Lyons looked to his partners, then turned back to the congressman. "What? What can I do for you?"

"When you find those who killed my friend—" Chris Buckley's hand closed into a fist "—do justice."

16

As Blancanales piloted the borrowed motor home south from San Francisco, Jefferson spun through the AM and FM radio stations. He paused to listen to news programs. Finally, he heard a report on the four killings:

"...investigators report the two men carried false identification. They had given an airport car-rental agency false names and identification. In what may be a related crime, two other men died this morning in a horrifying incident in the Twin Peaks area. Witnesses reported a number of gunmen firing weapons. Police refuse to link the killings last night and this morning, but they also refuse to comment on witnesses' statements indicating sawed-off shotguns were used in both shoot-outs...."

"You hear that?" Jefferson asked Lyons.

"You're famous." Lyons did not pause as he searched the interior of the motor home.

"I hope not...."

Standing feet apart to brace himself against the sway of the moving vehicle, Lyons had begun his search with the drawers of a kitchen cabinet converted to a desk. The furnishings and decor of the coach indicated Prescott used the thirty-foot-long vehicle not for vacations but for precinct work. The sink and enclosed toilet and the rear bedroom remained, but the aide had remodeled the motor home to reflect his European taste in design. Gray industrial linoleum covered the floor. Curtains had been replaced with pull-down shades. White sheet plastic covered the walls. Steel and cloth folding chairs replaced all the couches and bucket seats. Wall-mounted telephones lacked only connecting lines to create a self-contained political office. With the breakfast table and couches gone, the interior became almost spacious.

Lyons pulled out the first drawer. It contained pens, pencils, felt markers, and the congressman's letterhead stationery and envelopes. Lyons examined every pen and eraser, then looked at the underside of the drawer.

"What you doing, Ironman?" Gadgets called out from the bedroom. The Stony Man electronics specialist had spread out all of his equipment on the fold-out double bed. "You think those liberals put a bomb on board?"

"No. Maybe a microphone. Maybe a cassette recorder."

Jefferson swiveled around. He sat in the second bucket seat immediately next to Blancanales, who was driving. "Bob wouldn't do that. He's a good guy. Ricardo, he and I were like brothers."

"Marquez was a reporter, right?" Lyons asked. "And you're a reporter?"

"When I can get the work."

"Did Prescott give you stories?"

"Sure. The congressman's Mr. Conspiracy himself. Always investigating something."

"Well, no one's going to be reading about *us* in the newspapers." Lyons set the drawer aside and pulled out another. He examined rolls of sealing tape and wrapping paper.

"But they're with us," Jefferson protested. "They won't go public on us."

"They would if they got the chance. That's why I shot off my mouth like I did. They were so smooth, I just had to hear what they really thought. And the congressman told me."

Blancanales glanced back to Lyons. "Indeed. The man told you to 'do justice.' I think you made a convert to the cause."

"Maybe. But while Buckley gave me his speech, that Prescott goof was outside. And I don't know what he was doing."

"Is he ever paranoid!" Gadgets shouted forward to Blancanales. "Now he thinks Congress is trying to get us?"

Disregarding his partner's joking, Lyons continued his search. He went through the other drawers, setting each aside after he checked the contents. Then he examined the interior of the cabinet, shining a flashlight inside. Where he could not see, he explored with his fingertips.

"If you wait a minute," Gadgets told him, "I'll do an electronic sweep."

"That's not good enough. What if it's just a cassette recorder? What if it's one of those radio-switched units?"

"Go to it. Then I'll give it a sweep. We'll see what kind of equipment Congress has got."

As they left San Francisco behind, the morning commuter traffic thinned. The urban and manufacturing areas gave way to the suburbs of San Mateo, San Carlos, Palo Alto, then the city of San Jose. Blancanales maintained a steady sixty miles per hour. Other motor homes passed, the travelers—families or retired people—waving. Blancanales and Jefferson returned the greetings. Lyons continued his search, tapping the walls, looking inside the burners of the stove. Gadgets glanced out the back window from time to time, watching for cars following the motor home.

Jefferson wandered back to the bedroom. He saw Able Team's equipment and weapons.

"Oh, my God. I thought you guys just had pistols, like normal people." He pointed at the Atchisson full-auto shotgun. "What in hell is that?"

"A shotgun," Gadgets answered.

"Looks like a machine gun."

"It's a selective-fire twelve-gauge shotgun," Lyons told him. "Semi-auto, three shot, and full-auto. Not exactly a pocket weapon, but where it goes, the bad guys die."

"And those pistols. They have silencers."

"You guessed it," Gadgets said as he finally activated his counterelectronic unit. The hand-held device used magnetic fields to detect transmitters. Gadgets worked his way through the motor home, waving the long oval antenna inside every cabinet and closet, over every surface and piece of furniture.

"Nothing."

Lyons went forward to Blancanales. "Next turnoff,

we park for a while. I'd like to get under this barge. See if anything's on the undercarriage."

"It'll cost us time."

"This is not Team equipment. I won't go any further without completing the checkout."

Two miles farther on, Blancanales pulled off at a roadside rest station. Three other motor homes and campers were parked near the picnic tables. A family from Ohio cooked breakfast under the canvas awning of their trailer, ignoring the freeway's noise and smog. Blancanales drove past them and parked at the far end of the area.

Stripping off his sport coat, Lyons unbuckled his shoulder holster and Colt Python. He took his flashlight and Gadgets's counterelectronic wand.

"Want to come supervise?" Lyons asked Gadgets.

"As long as I don't have to get dirty."

"Specialist!" Lyons muttered sarcastically.

He started at the front bumper. Then on his back on the asphalt, he searched the interior of the stamped steel bumper with his fingers. He heard a tone coming from the counterelectronic wand. Gadgets dropped flat to peer under the motor home.

"What did you find?"

"Didn't find anything. It just buzzed."

"You drop it?"

"I just laid it down while I crawled under here."

Hammering slammed the motor home's aluminum siding. Both men recognized the zip-crack of high-velocity slugs. Glass shattered.

Their reflexes threw them into motion as Blancanales started the diesel engine again. Gadgets grabbed the door handle as the motor home lurched into motion.

Lyons trotted alongside as Blancanales maneuvered through the parking lot. A Piper Club circled above them at a few hundred feet. Squinting against the morning sun, Lyons saw the dark triangle of the plane's open side-door. A point of light flashed one-two-three, then three slugs punched into the motor home. The freeway noise drowned out the reports of the auto-rifle.

Lyons swung inside. "There's a plane up above us. Rifleman firing from the passenger side."

Bits of white plastic and urethane foam exploded from the ceiling. In the bedroom, Gadgets pressed tight the Velcro closures on his Kevlar and steel-plate battle armor. Lyons rushed to the equipment, and Gadgets handed him his battle armor.

Lyons pushed it away. "Put it on, Floyd. He's the witness we're protecting." He slipped on his shoulder holster and Python, then buckled on a bandolier of box magazines for his Atchisson selective-fire assault shotgun.

"Up front!" Blancanales shouted, steering as he sealed his armor's closures.

Setting the Atchisson's safety, Lyons snapped back the actuator to strip the first twelve-gauge round off the magazine. The motor home lurched as he ran forward. Lyons staggered, fell against the driver's bucket seat as a line of slugs smashed the windshield.

Through the patterns of shatter-crazed safety glass, Lyons saw two gunmen with Uzis scrambling from a rusted, dented Plymouth station wagon. The gunmen—black men in jeans and flowing African shirts, their hair ratted into globes—took cover behind the Plymouth as the driver leveled a shotgun through the passenger-side window.

Lyons jammed the fourteen-inch barrel of the Atchisson through the shattered windshield and thumbed the weapon's fire-selector all the way forward.

A storm of high-velocity steel shot swept the old station wagon. Handloaded by the Stony Man weaponsmith, Andrzej Konzaki, each twelve-gauge shell packed a mix of fifty number-two and double-ought steel balls, a mixture developed and proved in the jungle wars of Malaysia by British counterinsurgency commandos. Unlike lead shot, the steel shot did not deform or flatten when it struck objects or flesh. An automobile's thin sheet metal did not deflect or absorb the balls.

Glass exploded, plastic shattered, brains and blood sprayed in clouds as a three-round burst—one hundred fifty steel projectiles—found the first gunman where he crouched at the Plymouth's rear bumper. His head and right arm gone, blood foaming from his yawning chest cavity, the dead man flew back, his pocked and gory Uzi clattering across the access road.

Two blasts found the driver, the first round's high-velocity steel punching through the passenger door to jerk him upright, the spent balls smashing his hands and face, bloodying the gunman but not killing him. The second round, velocity undiminished by the auto's sheet steel, passed through the open passenger window and tore his head away.

Looking over the Atchisson's sights, Lyons saw the

third gunman glance over at the headless body of his comrade, the nerve spasms of the blood-spurting corpse jerking the arms and torso in fish-flops. Lyons put the last two rounds of the mag into the third man's chest and head. Another suddenly headless dead man went flopping to hell.

The Atchisson's action locked back. Lyons dropped out the empty magazine and took another from his bandolier.

Blancanales had snatched a double-edged knife from a sheath on his left ankle as he drove, and he slashed at the plastic and shattered glass of the windshield. He saw another car carrying black men with Uzis fishtail from the freeway.

"Hit them!" Blancanales pointed with the blade.

Before the gunmen could throw open the doors of their red Cadillac, Jefferson's sawed-off Smith & Wesson boomed, a load of number-six lead birdshot annihilating the windshield and spraying the interior of the Cadillac with bits of glass. The young reporter tromboned the slide and fired again, the lightweight birdshot wounding the driver. As Jefferson worked the slide to fire again, Lyons's assault-shotgun raked the enemy's car.

Straining against the weapon's jackhammering recoil, Lyons held the muzzle on line as steel shot slammed the hood, windshield and interior. Blood and flesh splashed over the upholstery as the full-auto fire shredded the four gunmen.

Blancanales accelerated past the demolished Cadillac. In the back, Gadgets saw a dying gunman stagger from the car. One arm hung limp, blood was bubbling from a pattern of holes in his chest, but he still gripped an Uzi. One-handed, he raised the 9mm submachine gun to avenge himself.

Sighting his CAR-15 on the gunman, Gadgets fired through the rear window. Tempered glass sprayed both inward and outward as Gadgets triggered one burst, then another, then another. Deflected by the glass, the first burst skipped off the asphalt and banged the Cadillac, only one slug punching through the already dying man's chest. But the second and third bursts knocked him back, slugs tearing away his jaw and forehead as he staggered back, finally dead.

Slugs from the rifleman in the plane above them continued to punch through the roof of the motor home. Meanwhile all in the vehicle heard the continued buzzing of Gadgets's electronic detector.

Peering through the shattered windshield, Blancanales swerved into the freeway traffic. Gadgets ran forward with the droning detector. He adjusted a dial, then waved the unit over the floor of the motor home.

Near the gas and brake pedals, at the point nearest the front bumper, the detector buzzed. As he backed away, the buzzing stopped. He told the others. "We got D.F. up front here. Must be radio-switched. That's why I didn't find it before."

"Prescott!" Lyons cursed. "That pink shit!"

Blancanales glanced into the rearview mirror. "Quit the talk, Ironman. We got two more cars gaining on us."

Slugs from the plane punched through the roof. Auto-fire from the pursuing cars hammered the back of the motor home. Slugs tore through the interior.

Lyons slapped another magazine into his Atchisson. He crouchwalked through the wrecked interior of the mobile political office.

"Prescott's going to get it."

Gadgets followed a step behind him. "Not if we get it first."

Hurrying past the few patrons having breakfast, legislative aide Bob Prescott went to the pay phone at the rear of the fashionable café in the financial district of San Francisco. He pulled a handful of dimes and quarters from his pocket. Punching a long series of numbers, he then dropped in three dollars in coins.

"Good afternoon, sir. You've heard the news. Your men failed.... The ones last night and this morning.... No sir, he won't escape."

The stylish young attorney glanced to the nearest tables. A man and a woman spread a fanfolded computer printout on the table. The man, in a tie-dyed shirt blazing with a hundred colors, his thinning blond hair in a long ponytail, totaled figures on a briefcase-sized computer. The woman, in a conservative gray suit, explained the significance of several lines on the printout. Neither the man nor the woman had any interest in the man a few steps away speaking into the pay phone.

"They won't escape.... The reporter told me he has the photographs and negatives on him. So they will burn with him.... I activated the units I held in reserve, the mercenaries...no, not your countrymen, no one will link these soldiers to your country. That black journalist Jefferson will die. I'm using blacks to kill a black."

Weaving through the light traffic, the two cars of black gunmen used trucks and passenger cars as shields. Unwilling to risk killing innocent drivers, Gadgets and Lyons held their fire. Above them, the rifleman continued firing down through the motor home's roof.

Lyons watched slugs punch through the ceiling. Bits of plastic and bullet fragments rattled on the linoleum floor. He picked up a deformed fragment of 5.56mm slug.

"If they had an M-60 up there," Lyons yelled, passing the slug to Gadgets, "we'd be closed down."

An impact showered them with plastic. Setting his CAR-15 on semi-automatic, Gadgets sighted on the plane above them with his CAR-15.

Firing carefully aimed shots, Gadgets emptied the short assault rifle's magazine. Appearing unaffected, the plane made no attempt to evade his fire. Slugs continued punching through the roof.

Gadgets dropped out the magazine, jammed in another. He flicked the fire-selector to full-auto. To correct for the sixty-mile-per-hour crosswind, he aimed ahead of the Piper Cub. He fired the entire magazine, thirty brass cartridge casings showering Lyons.

The Piper veered away.

"Think I got it?" Gadgets asked.

Lyons did not answer. Startled by the rifle fire from the motor home, a commuter two lanes to the left had hit her brakes and swerved to the shoulder. Her panic exposed the nearest car of gunmen. Lyons sighted on its windshield. He fired a three-shot burst of twelve-gauge rounds.

At the same instant, Uzi-fire from the car hammered the left side of the motor home, the 9mm slugs tearing through the aluminum siding and exiting through the other side.

One hundred fifty steel balls traveling at 1,200 feet per second hit the pursuing car. The gunner in the front seat died instantly. Though the windshield deflected many of the projectiles, a spray of blood and the car's sudden lurch to the side indicated that Lyons had hit the driver.

Lyons sighted again on the weaving car. He saw a man in the back seat struggle to shove the bloody driver aside. Lyons fired as the car swerved across two lanes, the steel shot smashing a headlight, pocking a fender. He sighted to fire again, but the car sideswiped a pickup truck. The truck's tires smoked as the driver panic-braked. Both the car and the truck skidded to a stop.

Blancanales changed lanes. Slugs exploded through the motor home's right side. Accelerating from behind a diesel truck and trailer, two black gunmen strafed the motor home. As Gadgets and Lyons shifted positions to fire, the driver hit his brakes to regain the cover of the diesel.

Looking down from the high cab of the semi, the

driver saw the ongoing firefight. He spoke into a citizens band microphone as he slowed his truck to get out of the line of fire.

Running through the litter of broken glass and plastic, Lyons went to a side window. He called back to Gadgets, "When the truck slows, they'll—"

"There they are!" Gadgets shouted back.

The gunmen's car accelerated, two Uzi muzzles extended from the back window of the driver's side. Lyons flipped his fire-selector to full-auto and aimed low. Gadgets fired first, the burst of high-velocity 5.56mm slugs from his CAR-15 destroying the skull of one gunman, spraying flesh from the shoulder and arm of the second man.

Lyons triggered a long burst of full-auto twelve-gauge fire. He swept the entire length of the old Chevrolet with steel, hammering sheet steel, tearing apart the whitewalls of the tires, a thousand fragments of flesh and bone and glittering glass exploding from the opposite side of the car as a dying gunman and the rear window disintegrated.

Careering wildly, the Chevy hit the bumper of the diesel. Metal screamed as the huge truck pushed the automobile sideways at fifty miles per hour. Tires smoking, the diesel braked, launching the Chevy into a roll. Doors flew open, the gyrating car throwing corpses to the asphalt. Flames came in a whirl of orange.

"One down!" yelled Lyons.

Slugs threw papers and pens from a shattered drawer as he went to the other side of the motor home.

The first car—the three surviving gunmen firing:

two men from the back seat; the driver steering with one hand and squeezing off pistol shots with his other—gained speed. Jefferson's Smith & Wesson shotgun boomed.

Glass showered Blancanales as slugs shattered the picture window. The stocky Puerto Rican jerked sideways as a slug punched through the sidewall and hit the Kevlar of his battle armor.

"You all right?" Lyons called out.

"Shut up and shoot!" Blancanales shouted back.

Tearing another magazine from his bandolier, Lyons loaded and sighted. He fired a single round at the gunmen firing from the rear seat. The torso of one man exploded.

Lyons glanced at the magazine he had loaded. Not buckshot, but one-ounce slugs. Custom-fabricated by Konzaki, the slugs contained tungsten-steel cores for penetrating steel or Kevlar armor. He aimed next at the front fender as Gadgets's CAR-15 wounded another gunman. Lyons fired again and again.

Huge dents appeared in the fender as the steel-cored slugs hit with the foot-pound impact of express trains. A tire shrieked as impact-deformed sheet metal cut into the sidewall. The driver fought for control of the car. Lyons put another slug through the windshield.

An arm flew from the car. With a dying man at the wheel, the car sideswiped the concrete-and-steel center divider and scraped to an eventual stop.

Gadgets and Lyons reloaded their weapons. Searching the freeway lanes behind them, they saw no pursuers. Victory.

But their attackers had almost destroyed them. Slip

wind blew through a hundred holes in the motor home. Every window had been shattered.

In the front, Jefferson reloaded his sawed-off shotgun. Blood trickled from a speckle pattern of tiny wounds on his face and left arm.

Lyons rushed to the young man. He examined the small wounds. A shard of glass protruded from one, a gleaming bit of bullet fragment from another.

"I'm okay, I'm all right," Jefferson told Lyons. He shrugged away Lyons's hands.

Lyons turned to Blancanales. "Where were you hit? You bleeding?"

"Take care of yourself," Gadgets told Lyons. "You're the one who's bloody."

"What?" Lyons wiped his hand across his forehead. His palm felt warm blood.

Blancanales looked to his partners. "I pronounce this vehicle a wreck. Time to get off the highway and find a replacement."

"Second the motion," Gadgets agreed. "Highway Patrol will catch up with us any minute now."

"State park five miles," Blancanales told them. He coasted through the curve of an off ramp.

"Think we can get this past the Rangers?" Lyons looked around at the bullet-destroyed motor home; glass continued falling from shattered windows as urethane dust from the walls' insulation blew in the wind.

"Spray paint, man," Gadgets told them. "What we need is some spray paint."

"What are you talking about?" Lyons demanded, incredulous.

"Vandals, *ese*," Gadgets jived in mock barrio dialect. "We stopped and we got vandalized. We're just tourists. We go to the wrong neighborhood, see what happen? *No bueno*."

As farms and roadside vegetable stands flashed past, Lyons leaned from the shattered picture window. High in the sky above them, he saw sunlight glint from the wings of a small plane.

"Wizard, we got a plane over us. Is that transmitter or whatever still on?"

Gadgets waved the electronic transmission detector over the front end of the motor home. The unit buzzed. "Got to stop. Pull that thing off. Either they got a D.F. on us or they're monitoring highway noise."

Lyons shook his head. "We'll leave it on. That way they can find us."

19

Captain Alejandro Madrano of *Organización Democrática Nacionalista*, better known by its acronym, ORDEN, watched the familiar landscape of central California flash past his car. Years before, after his training at Fort Bragg, he had visited his sister at the University of Southern California. He and his sister had toured California and Nevada for a week, visiting San Francisco, Yosemite and Reno. The decadence, the racial impurity, the weakness of the governing forces had enraged him. He had asked his sister:

"Why does this country, this cesspool of socialism and racial chaos, have the arrogance to meddle in the affairs of El Salvador?"

His sister had explained to him, in her innocence and ignorance, that what he saw represented "the freedoms of the North Americans."

But now he returned. With the help of the North Americans, he would battle the cultural sickness of this vast nation so that sickness would not condemn El Salvador to revolution. Today, they would exterminate the negro journalist and the three mercenaries protecting him from justice.

His driver spoke into the radio, communicating with the other drivers in the convoy of three Chevrolet Silverados. The electronics technician in the last truck reported a steady signal from the location device on the enemy's vehicle. Though the spotter plane had returned for refueling, the pilot's last report confirmed the position of the enemy.

Seated around him, his soldiers appeared to be businessmen touring California. They did not fear any encounter with the local authorities.

He and his soldiers carried the correct immigration stamps in their passports. They carried receipts proving they had rented the truck. Garbed in white suits and ties purchased from expensive shops in Miami and Beverly Hills, they only appeared to be tourists. Up until the moment they took their weapons from the packing cases stacked in the back of the Silverado, he and his soldiers would maintain their act as a group of prosperous Hispanics lavishing dollars on a visit to California.

Though his friends in the United States government had provided both materiel and moral support, Captain Madrano had no confidence in the North American people. Democrats, liberals, technocrats, Christians, Jews, whatever the word: all were Communist sympathizers.

Did not most North Americans belong to unions? Did they not applaud the Marxist movie actors in Hollywood? Did they not abandon General Somoza to the Sandinistas? Did not their corporations solicit business with the Russians and Red Chinese? Did they not contribute to the International Red Cross?

Though a responsible administration now ruled in Washington, the Communists controlled the news

media. Inundated with lies, the North American people—already in sympathy with the international communist conspiracy—opposed their leaders' efforts to battle the agents of the conspiracy.

If a North American policeman became too inquisitive, Captain Madrano's soldiers had orders to neutralize the threat immediately.

If a North American witnessed their attack on the Communists, his soldiers would eliminate the witness.

Although he did not have the express approval of the American president or the State Department officials who had processed his entry into the United States, Captain Madrano knew they would not disapprove. Had the administration prosecuted the killers of North Americans in El Salvador?

After three years, the "investigation" into the murder of three nuns and a church worker continued. After two and one-half years, the "investigation" into the murders of two American lawyers continued. After a year, the "investigation" into the murder of an American tourist continued.

With the cooperation of the United States government, attorneys and private investigators and family members visited El Salvador to demand justice. With the cooperation of the United States government, the Salvadoran "investigations" into the rapes and tortures and murders continued. The "investigations" would continue forever. . . .

Without convictions.

In fact, when Captain Madrano visited the Miami home of Colonel Quesada, the commander of *Los*

Guerreros Blancos, the colonel introduced him to two officers of the Federal Bureau of Investigation.

Two years before, Colonel Quesada had walked into the dining room of a San Salvador hotel and pointed out two North American labor lawyers—actually Communist agitators—sitting at a table with a Salvadoran Communist traitor. The colonel's soldiers then executed all the Communists.

After unrelenting agitation on the part of the Communist media and the Communist sympathizers in the American Congress, Captain Madrano had had to issue warrants for the arrest of Colonel Quesada and his officers. The colonel then took sanctuary in Miami, under the protection of friends in the Administration.

As an officer in the Salvadoran Army and ORDEN, Captain Madrano had fought the enemy in all its forms. He had become aware of the insidious nature of subversion at the party celebrating his sixteenth birthday. He and several friends from his military academy had taken one of his family's maids into a back room and had amused themselves for an hour. The teenage maid died during the rape. Concealed by darkness, he and his friends had dragged the body to a car and dumped it outside the city.

The next day, the maid's father attempted to break through the gates of the family estate. Madrano knew he had been betrayed. Despite the privilege of working for one of the best Spanish families in San Salvador, despite the family's generosity, one of the servants had betrayed the boys to the old Indian.

He had often heard his father rave about the impertinence of the Indians and *ladinos campesinos* who labored on the family's coffee plantations. On his birthday, because a worthless girl died during a game, the family's trusted domestic servants had betrayed him. Fortunately his father always posted soldiers at the gate or the Indian might have injured the young Madrano. The senior Madrano laughed at the incident. "Finally you are a man!"

Wealth guaranteed Alejandro Madrano a commission in the army of El Salvador. After graduating from a private academy, he entered the officers' school for training in command and protocol. However, he received his actual training in the mountain provinces, serving with army battalions fighting Communist bandits.

Why bother searching the mountains for the bandits when the *campesinos* who fed the Communists camped near the roads? His superior officers showed the young lieutenant how to simultaneously deny the bandits information and support: kill the *campesinos*. Kill anyone who saw the bandits and did not report what they saw to the authorities. Kill anyone who might have seen the bandits and not reported. Kill anyone in the area where the bandits operated.

As his commanders told him: Communism spreads like a disease; kill the carriers, and the disease dies.

Later, Lieutenant Madrano volunteered to fight with ORDEN. Thus he learned how to fight Communism in the fetid breeding grounds of the slums.

When the Communists and their sympathizers—the union agitators, the schoolteachers, the health workers—met to discuss their radical plans for taking power and wealth from the government, informers noted every name and memorized the faces.

In the night, with a few trustworthy men, Lieutenant Madrano cruised the avenues in one of the high-powered Dodges donated by the United States. They took the Communists from their homes and made examples of them.

Somehow, the death squads never succeeded in eradicating the contagion, even as vultures feasted at garbage dumps stinking with rotting human flesh, and roadside ditches buzzed with iridescent green carrion flies, and unrecognizable masses of bloated gray flesh floated in the shallows of Lago de Ilopango.

The voices of the scum continued in their demands for democracy, opportunity and justice. So the *escuadrones de muerte* organized into larger units. As army companies sealed off the barrios, the lieutenant and his compatriots used troop trucks to seize entire families.

In the barracks, the squad members' sexual amusements with the youths often proved to be the most effective interrogation technique. The screams of a youngster receiving first the lust of his soldiers, then the penetration of their knives would win names of co-conspirators from the parents when pliers and welding torches failed. Then the families joined the anonymous dead in the pits.

For his distinguished record in breaking a conspiracy among a union of truck drivers, teachers and nurses to create a meeting hall disguised as a children's health-care center, Lieutenant Madrano received his promotion to captain. His new duties included the administration of the land-reform program of the junta.

In the jeans and T-shirt of a student radical, he visited the new cooperatives dictated into existence by the much-publicized land-reform acts. With smiles and smooth words, he persuaded the farmers to elect leaders. He posed with the leaders while North American and European journalists photographed the scenes for their newspapers, magazines and television programs.

Once the journalists left, ORDEN executed the peasant leaders.

However, as the Communists stepped up the guerrilla war in the provinces, Captain Madrano refused any more assignments outside of San Salvador. He had no interest in the dirt and danger of combat. Let the draftees and North American soldiers fight in the remote fields and mountains. The captain continued his night war against subversion, drinking and dancing in the discos of the capital, then cruising the slums to find teenage Communist girls to interrogate.

Now he had the honor of carrying the war to the North American Communists. His duty in the United States offered him new opportunities. Today, as ordered, he would kill the journalist and his bodyguards. When would he receive orders to interrogate student radicals?

He thought of the blond coeds of USC and UCLA. As he shopped for gifts to send his mother in Spain, he had eyed the beautiful young girls strolling the campus in their shorts and tight jeans and miniskirts. Obviously whores. The posters announcing rallies against the United States intervention in El Salvador excited him. He hoped his commanders—in alliance with the Amer-

ican FBI—would assign him to the eradication of
Communist subversives from the universities. He
knew the pleasures of torturing and degrading Salvadoran girls. What pleasures would the American
blondes give him?

Already he had launched a campaign that was highly
unusual by any standards of international assassina-
tion. He had devised and executed a series of hits
against targets the American public despised. Thus his
mystery kill squads had earned a measure of tacit
popular support, the better to let them continue their
real work against refugees in the barrios and intellectuals in the universities.

With the help of smuggled-in troops from *El Ejercito de los Guerreros Blancos* and *Organización
Democrática Nacionalista*, and some of the more
determined hit men from *El Falange* and *La
Guardia*—and with funds supplied by the American
rich, transferred from the Treasury to Swiss bank ac-
counts—Madrano had engineered the executions of
rapists, murderers, other criminal targets who wandered into the fire zone from the revolving door of
America's "bleeding heart" justice system.

Throughout the United States the executions had
continued unchecked. In recent days the assassinations
had included two TV news personalities who had
spoken out against the earlier killings, plus a black nationalist and two other black agitators who were
known to be independently investigating the presence,
according to witnesses, of "Panthers" and "Mus-
lims" in the mystery death squads.

Reaction in the United States had ranged from horror at the wave of killings, to relief that the killings did in fact dispose of more career criminals than obvious innocents; this because the high-profile murders leached all the public's attention away from the vastly more extensive killings of unknown and uncared-about targets in the slums.

Madrano relished the uniqueness of the enterprise, ran over the details again in his mind.

His death squads had appeared to be intent on blowing away known psychos and troublemakers. They had carved a deliberate and bloody path through the hopeless bureaucratic garbage that clogged the U.S. courts. The American people appreciated such a task, though they might not want to admit it. And so a crisis of sorts was brewing in this so-called democracy, this festering Communist "free world"; law and order had been hijacked to work against the state. America was about to be turned against itself...cop against cop...leader against leader.... The laws and the law courts were being turned on their collective asses, just so that the killings could continue. Ha!

A change in speed jarred him from his fantasies. His driver left the freeway. The three-truck convoy passed fields and orchards. After a few miles, the flat landscape became hills covered with winding rows of fruit trees. Pines grew on the higher slopes. Finally his driver turned to him.

"Captain. The Communists are ahead. The plane reports their vehicle parked on a side road in the hills. We approach the road. What are your orders?"

"Load weapons. The pilot gave you precise directions?"

"Yes. He circled the area to confirm every detail. He saw them attempting to repair—"

"Then we speed to the Communists. We take them by surprise."

"Yes, Captain!" The driver relayed the instructions to the other two trucks.

Minutes later, the driver pointed to a dirt lane intersecting the highway. The road cut through orchards, then twisted into the foothills. Captain Madrano, an Uzi submachine gun in his hands, told the driver:

"The other trucks go first. Tell them to speed."

Following the driver's directions, two Silverados accelerated through the orchards, dust clouding behind them. Captain Madrano's driver followed a moment later. Hurtling through the swirling dust at fifty miles per hour, the trucks wove along the road.

Steep hills rose on both sides. Cattle trails cut the dry weeds. Here and there, green brush dotted the hillsides. A voice squawked from the walkie-talkie.

"Captain. We see the truck."

"Park and then surround it! Soon we execute the Communists!"

Captain Madrano saw the two leading trucks swerve, one to the right, the other to the left. They both came to a halt, and then his men rushed from the trucks.

Their enemy had parked in a fold of the hillsides. Earth movers had leveled an area. To one side, ramps constructed of heavy timbers provided for the loading of produce trucks. Around the scraped area, trucks had flattened the weeds. Tire-rutted mud had hardened under the sun. Beyond, the hillsides rose at a forty-five-degree angle. Captain Madrano knew he had the journalist and his Communist guards trapped. There could be no escape.

As his driver stopped the Silverado, Captain Madrano waited for the first shots. His men climbed from the truck and joined the other Salvadorans circling the motor home. The captain stayed to the rear, his Uzi in one hand, the walkie-talkie in the other.

His men closed the circle. A soldier called out, *"¡Putos comunistas. Venimos con muerte!"*

Then came the first shot. The soldier who promised death dropped dead.

A storm of death engulfed them all

20

From the safety of concealment on the hillside overlooking the motor home, Floyd Jefferson watched as the three "specialists from Washington" prepared for the death squad. Though he did not know their real names, he already thought of the three men as friends. No, more than friends—brothers.

He knew their assignment: Protect the young American reporter who may be the only surviving witness to an international Fascist conspiracy of murder and mutilation.

Protect Floyd Jefferson!

After they had left the highway, they found this isolated canyon. While the plane circled overhead, they went through the pretense of repairing the motor home. Finally, after the plane disappeared to the north, they took their positions. The "specialists" refused to allow Jefferson to participate. To force him to remain safe, they had tried to take away his sawed-off shotgun. He refused and argued until they allowed him to keep it. From the hillside, he watched their hurried preparations.

The man he had heard the others call "Pol," who had identified himself to Jefferson over the phone as Rosario, moved through the low weeds. He paused from time to time in the thickest tangles of brush, then moved on to the loading ramp of heavy timbers.

The "Wizard" assembled a device and placed it on the hillside. Jefferson had never been in the army. He had no idea what the "Wizard" had devised.

"Ironman," the rude blond bastard, buckled on the heavy black body armor that Jefferson had worn during the freeway pursuit. Weapons and ammunition overlay the armor. With his "machine-gun" shotgun and two pistols, the man looked terrifying. A pair of sunglasses and a crazy grin made him look like Mr. Death himself.

These three "specialists" knew their job. They had parked the motor home in a V formed by two steep hillsides. Rosario and Ironman took positions at each side of the opening. The Wizard waited at the point of the V. Jefferson knew the death squad would have no chance.

These men were true warriors, not farmers with machetes for self-defense. Not students. Not nurses waiting at a bus stop. Not teachers at a blackboard.

The Salvadoran monsters faced qualified "specialists": death squad against death squad. Except this death squad of North American soldiers fought for justice.

Finally, three trucks arrived. As dust clouds swirled across the clearing, squads of men spread out. A Salvadoran from the third truck directed his men with a walkie-talkie. One of the Salvadorans shouted out: *"¡Putos comunistas. Venimos con muerte!"*

In a roar of automatic weapons, justice struck the Salvadorans.

GADGETS FIRED FIRST from his position on the hillside. Sighting over the short barrel of his CAR, he put three-round bursts into the chests of the two nearest Salvadorans. They fell back and writhed in the dust, blood fountaining from their hearts. Gadgets put his commando-rifle sights onto another gunman staring around for the source of the auto-fire. An Uzi in his hands, the gunman stood exposed in the kill zone. A three-round burst punched through his head, his questions and indecision suddenly a red mist in the midday glare.

The other Salvadorans scattered. Bursts of 9mm slugs from their Uzis whizzed into the sky as they sprayed fire. Dust puffed on the hillside. Glass broke in the motor home from the wild, unaimed auto-fire.

Aimed bursts from Lyons and Blancanales knocked down Salvadorans, every burst throwing dead and wounded to the gravel.

A wounded man screamed, his cry rising and falling, auto-blasts drowning his agony. Gadgets ignored the thrashing man and searched the area for men still firing. From his position above the clearing, he looked down on the Salvadorans. They had no shelter other than the motor home and the shallow gully at the base of the hillside.

Two gunmen sprinted from the clearing and plunged into the gully. Gadgets watched them cower behind the rocks. He suppressed a laugh.

Who were these goofs? They could write an encyclopedia on how to die in an ambush. Then again, they wouldn't have time.

The Stony Man electronics technician extended his

hand for the radio-trigger. But he did not press the button.

Why blast only two? Wait for a crowd....

A Salvadoran ran for the road. Something snagged on his ankle. He glanced back, saw a grenade bouncing after him. Shrieking with panic, he sprinted. But the grenade, secured by a loop of monofilament to his ankle, followed only a step behind.

The sharp crack of RDX stopped his shriek for a moment. Stumbling, dropping his Uzi, the gunman attempted to get to his feet. He no longer had feet.

Screaming, the maimed Salvadoran thrashed on the hard-baked earth. Blood gushed from the stumps of his legs, blood loss plunging him into shock. His scream died to a whimper, then a gasp. Finally he lay silent and motionless, flies buzzing around the exposed knobs of his tibias and fibulas.

Lyons wanted prisoners. Therefore he aimed low. He sighted on running Salvadorans, tore their legs apart. Though most of them would bleed to death, perhaps one or two might live for interrogation.

Another Salvadoran dodged through the cross fire to the gully. There, the other two gunmen aimed fire at the hillside brush that concealed Gadgets. Lyons snapped two blasts from his Atchisson at the men in the gully to keep their heads down, then he returned his attention to the clearing.

Two Salvadorans took cover under the motor home. Shielded from the downward directed fire from Gadgets and Blancanales, the two gunmen sought out Lyons with their Uzis. Other Salvadorans scrambled under the protection of the motor home.

The Salvadorans formed into fire teams, one man aiming a quick short burst, then another firing, then another. A continuous stream of slugs kept Lyons down, Uzi-fire tearing the brush that concealed him.

Sprawled on his gut, the 9mm slugs from the Salvadorans passing only inches above his back, Lyons keyed his hand-radio.

"Pol! Do it!"

On the opposite hillside, Blancanales sighted his M-16/M-203 over-and-under hybrid assault rifle/grenade launcher on the motor home's shot-out rear picture window. He flicked down the M-203's safety. As he squeezed the trigger, another Salvadoran crawled under the shelter of the vehicle.

A 40mm high-explosive grenade flew through the window of the motor home. Inside, the explosion sent high-velocity steel razors through the floor, piercing the fuel tank in a hundred places. Gasoline sprayed the Salvadorans.

Drenched in gas, the gunmen scrambled from under the motor home. Blancanales reloaded and fired again, the second grenade hitting under the rear bumper. The nearest Salvadoran died instantly, steel wire razors slashing simultaneously through his lungs, heart and brain. The others did not share his good fortune.

Bursting into gas-fed flames, screaming, thrashing their arms wildly as if to shake away the agony consuming their flesh, the Salvadorans ran blindly in all directions. A wounded gunman, unable to crawl from under the burning motor home, wailed for thirty seconds, then sucked down a breath of fire and died choking, his lungs seared shut.

The burning men ran through the cross fire. Blancanales sighted on each suffering Salvadoran and gave them the mercy of a bullet. Lyons saved his steel buckshot for the Salvadorans still firing their weapons.

A gunman, his expensive suit torn, filthy, darted for the loading dock. Lyons followed him in his sights. He fired as the gunman dived. The blast of double-ought and number-two shot almost missed him, the majority of the fifty steel balls only tearing into the dust beyond him. But a few projectiles at the shot pattern's edge ripped his legs with through-and-through wounds, their impact twisting him in the air. He fell hard on his shoulder. Crabbing for the shelter of the loading dock's heavy timbers, the gunman left streams of blood on the hard-packed dirt and gravel.

In his desperation and pain, the Salvadoran did not see the monofilament line. The strand caught on his shoulder as he crawled.

The monofilament pulled an Italian-made MU-50G controlled-effect grenade from a cola can. Blancanales had learned to make this particular booby trap from the Viet Cong. Tie a wire or string to a grenade, pull the safety pin, then put the grenade in a can. The can prevented the safety lever from springing free. But when a soldier snagged the line, the line jerked the grenade from the can and the lever flipped away. Crude but effective. The delay of the grenade often worked to make the booby trap more effective. If a pointman on a trail snagged the line, the six-second delay gave time for the next man in the patrol to enter the kill-radius of the grenade. Shrapnel ripped the pointman's back, shrapnel ripped the gut of the next soldier.

However, in the case of the wounded Salvadoran, the six-second delay only served as a period of torture. As the man crawled against the dock, he felt the grenade fall on his back. He reached behind him, felt the shape of the small grenade. The soldier recognized the shape of it by touch.

He tried to grab the grenade. It rolled to his side. The guy struggled to crawl away. His wounded, blood-spurting legs kicked at the dirt and weeds. As in a nightmare, he saw the grenade at his side, yet he could not crawl away. Dropping his Uzi, the victim clawed at the earth, dragging himself a few feet. He did not feel the monofilament looped over his shoulder.

The grenade followed him. He kicked at it, his eyes bulging from his face, his face distorted into a mask of terror. Then the grenade exploded.

Designated a "controlled-effect" grenade because the tiny explosive charge of the MU-50G created a kill-radius of only five meters—thus making it an excellent anti-personnel grenade for clearing rooms of terrorists—the blast did not have the force to kill the man instantly. However, the explosive shock and hundreds of steel beads hit his legs at a speed of 20,000 feet per second, tearing away his legs and genitals.

Flopping in the rapidly spreading pool of his blood, the guy did not understand what had happened to him. But he screamed and screamed as his life drained away from the torn flesh that revealed his pelvic bones. In the last minute of his life he knew the horror he had inflicted on so many others. Then he sank into the darkness of unconsciousness and death.

Black smoke rising from the flaming motor home

shadowed the killing ground. Over the sights of their assault weapons, Blancanales and Lyons searched the area. They saw wounded and dead Salvadorans everywhere. A brushfire spread around one dead man as his gasoline-flaming body ignited the dry weeds.

Auto-fire still came from the three gunmen hiding in the rocky gully. Lyons scanned the killing ground. He counted three wounded men still moving. He keyed his hand-radio.

"Pol, give them the chance to surrender."

Blancanales shouted out in Spanish for the survivors to throw away their weapons.

Below, one of the men wounded by Lyons, flat on his back with his shattered legs twisted beneath him, raised his arms. Another man, his intestines spilling from his shirt, died even as he called for mercy. The third man, a broken arm limp at his side, waved one hand and stood.

An Uzi-burst from the Salvadorans in the gully killed him. Lyons spoke into his hand-radio again.

"Wizard, give those three the pop."

"Put out some rounds to distract them, then," said Gadgets's voice.

As Lyons sprayed the three Salvadorans with buckshot, Gadgets touched the radio-trigger at his side to send a radio impulse to a charge he had placed in the gully.

Much like the monofilament and grenade booby traps Blancanales had placed, the device Gadgets had improvised utilized a can and a grenade. However, Gadgets used a radio-triggered fuse—a tiny bit of RDX usually planted inside a brick of C-4 plastic explosive to ignite the main charge—to propel the grenade from the can.

As the steel shot from Lyons's booming Atchisson hit the rocks around them, the three Salvadorans stayed low, their faces against the earth. They did not notice the grenade propelled straight into the air by the tiny explosion of the fuse. A length of monofilament prevented the grenade from flying too far or bouncing away. When the grenade had flown to the end of its tether, it snapped back and clattered on the rocks among the men.

They died without seeing what killed them.

Gadgets laughed into his hand-radio. "Presto, deado."

"I'm going out there," Lyons radioed his partners. "Cover me."

Jamming a full magazine into his Atchisson, Lyons left his concealment on the hillside. His steps slow with the weight of the Kevlar-and-steel battle armor, he eased down the treacherous slope, his Atchisson cocked and unlocked and set on full-auto, his right index finger straight beside his Atchisson's trigger. He needed only to clench his fist to send a devastating blast of high-velocity steel from the weapon.

On the scraped earth of the loading area, Lyons scanned the dead and wounded. He saw several of the men he had wounded, now dead in immense pools of clotting blood.

Going to one of the Salvadorans who still lived, he kicked the man's Uzi away. Atchisson ready in his right hand, Lyons reached under the wounded man's jacket and pulled a Browning 9mm auto-pistol from a shoulder holster. Tossing the Browning aside, he glanced at the man's shattered legs. One leg bled from a pattern of buckshot holes. The other leg, the femur shattered, twisted at a right angle. Lyons keyed his hand-radio.

"Pol, this one needs immediate first aid."

"On my way."

21

Flat in the dust under the Silverado, Captain Madrano watched the black-clad North American walk away. The captain had lost all his men, but he still held his Uzi. He watched the other North Americans come down from the hillsides.

Could he kill them all with his Uzi? No. Perhaps he could kill one. No. Why throw away his life with a last, suicidal attack on the enemy?

Smoke from the burning motor home drifted through the clearing. Captain Madrano saw the smoke obscure the scene for a moment. The slight wind blew the black cloud past the Silverado. Madrano watched the three armored North Americans check the Salvadorans. The Negro stayed back at a safe distance.

Captain Madrano knew he had only one chance to live. He waited for the wind to shift again.

A gust blew the smoke one way, then the wind faded. A billowing black wall descended on the Silverados. Madrano slithered backward from under the truck. Keeping the truck between him and the North Americans, he scrambled back.

When he gained the cover of weeds and a tangle of litter dumped at the side of the road, he burrowed into the trash like an animal. Concealed, he waited until he heard one of the Silverados start up. Only after the North Americans departed did Captain Madrano dare to emerge into the daylight.

Throwing away his weapons, he walked to the highway, plotting revenge every step of the way.

22

As local and federal officers photographed the dead Salvadorans, Agent Gallucci of the Federal Bureau of Investigation surveyed the scene.

Stinking soot and smoke still rose from the ruin of the motor home, the aluminum frame and shell melted and commingled with the ashes of the interior materials.

Scorched human bones lay in the gleaming pools of once-molten iridescent aluminum. Farther away from the smoking hulk, more Salvadorans lay where they had died. As if to declare their identities, the corpses clutched their passports and tourist visas. Their killers had searched their pockets for the identification, then left the official documents in their stiffening hands.

Though the papers stated the young men represented a group of visiting Mexican businessmen, their hard muscles, their military-short hairstyles identified the dead men as soldiers or paramilitary fighters.

Their wounds left no doubt as to the military weapons of their killers. Dismembered by grenades, their heads and torsos torn open by auto-fire, the 5.56mm and 40mm cartridge casings found on the hillside only confirmed what Gallucci immediately recognized.

But the hideous wounds to some of the Salvadorans confused him. How could the gunman who killed the men—obviously with a shotgun—have chambered and fired shells so fast and with such devastating accuracy?

A farmer on the far side of the hill had reported hearing a fury of gunshots and explosions. Before he could cross his equipment yard to his telephone, the shooting stopped. The slaughter of these Salvadorans had taken no more than a few minutes.

The number of wounds in the dead men indicated continuous firing from a semi-automatic short-barreled weapon. No weapon Gallucci knew of could put out the sustained volume of fire indicated by the twenty-one shotgun casings on the hillside—all of a common manufacturer. Only the scratches on the casings' brass bases indicating an unusual extractor mechanism would provide the laboratory with any detail for analysis.

"Mr. Gallucci! Over here." One of the San Jose county sheriffs called him over to a Silverado truck.

"Look at this. . . ." The sheriff pointed to a pattern of holes in the passenger-side door.

Holes of .30 caliber and other holes not much larger than pinpoints created the outline of a man's legs. Chipped enamel indicated where other shot balls had lost velocity as they passed through the man's legs and only dented the truck's sheet steel. A trail of blood from the truck led to a corpse in the weeds.

Gallucci looked up at the hillside to confirm the angle of aim to the door panel. He examined the holes punched into the truck's steel.

The sheriff explained. "Only time I've seen buck-shot penetrate a car is point-blank, straight on. But look. I estimate twenty-five yards from where the shotgunner fired. At a twenty-something degree angle. But his pellets—looks like a mixed load, buckshot and bird shot—they went straight through the sheet metal. Except for where that Mexican was standing. And the shot went through him and still dented the door.''

"It'll give the lab something to think about," Gallucci told him.

"Me, too. Someone is running around who I don't want to meet."

Gallucci noticed marks in the dust of the road. As if continuing his search for more evidence, the FBI officer walked away from the county sheriff.

On the other side of the Silverado, handprints and the wider prints of knees indicated a man had crawled from under the truck to the other side of the road. Gallucci continued to the roadside. The handprints and scuffs showed where the escaping man had gained the concealment of weeds and trash. Footprints from the trash led toward the highway.

Gallucci glanced around at the other officers. They were combing the hillsides and killing ground. The Silverado blocked their view of him.

As if he only walked back and forth to examine the ground, Gallucci eradicated the marks of his Salvadoran brother-in-struggle who had escaped.

A sheriff called out, "Mr. Gallucci. We got a break!"

"What?" Gallucci walked to the sheriff's department patrol car.

"There's a gunshot case at the hospital."

"Let's go!" Gallucci ran for his bureau vehicle.

23

Flashing his Federal Bureau of Investigation identification to the admitting clerk, Agent Gallucci demanded: "I got a report of a gunshot case here. What room?"

Waiting outpatients and visitors crowded the reception room of San Jose County Hospital. A teenage candy striper wheeled a cart of magazines from couch to couch; a young man with a leg in a cast waved to get her attention. At the front desk, the clerk glanced at Gallucci's identification.

"Just a moment...." The white-haired clerk touch-coded an extension number. "What is the status of the Mexican man?" She listened for a moment, then turned to the agent.

"He's under sedation, sir. We're preparing an operating room for him now."

"Is he conscious?"

"In and out. He has a compound fracture of his left femur, shock from blood loss, serious gunshot wounds. I doubt if he could answer questions."

"Where did you find him?"

"In front of the hospital. Someone simply dumped him on the parkway. They had given him expert first aid, but—"

"What name did he give you?"

"That's a problem. The police tried to question him about that. His identification says he's from Mexico. On a business trip, but he told us he's Salvadoran. Kept begging us to call the State Department. The United States Department of State. Says he wants asylum. Is that why you're here?"

Gallucci nodded. "How long until he goes into surgery?"

"Soon."

"Well, I'll see what he has to say."

"Officer, he—"

"If he's conscious, we'll talk. If not, I'll come back tomorrow. What room?"

"Room 113. That doorway and to the right. Halfway down the hall."

Passing through the lobby, Gallucci glanced at the security guard posted at the side of the large room. The potbellied guard leaned against the wall watching the waiting area's television. Gallucci continued into the hallway. He noted that the food-service workers wore plain white uniforms without badges or identification tags.

Room 113 smelled of blood and antiseptic. The wounded Salvadoran opened his eyes as Gallucci went to the bed. Gallucci looked at the bandages covering the young man's body. He could not be the soldier who escaped.

"You are State Department?" the wounded young man asked.

Gallucci went to the room's bathroom. He looked inside, saw the door to the adjoining room open. No one occupied the other room. Gallucci pulled the door closed and locked it. Only then did he answer the Salvadoran.

"So you want asylum? Why?"

"I...have had enough of war and...killing. No more."

"War? What're you talking about? You're a Mexican. Mexico's not at war with us."

"I am Salvadoran.... My commander, Colonel Quesada...he ordered.... I come to kill North Americans."

"Who shot you?"

"North Americans. Why do you ask me that? I told them everything...."

"You mean the police?"

"Who shot me...who killed all the others...I told them everything...."

"So you're willing to cooperate?"

"Yes...I cooperate...."

"That's all I needed to know. *Adios, amigo.*"

Gallucci left the room quickly. He went to a pay phone in the lobby of the hospital and called a San Francisco number.

An hour after the young Salvadoran left surgery, a food-service worker entered his room. The worker pressed a pillow over the face of the Salvadoran.

His war had indeed ended.

24

Stepping over trash and bottles, Antonio Rivera descended the urine-stinking stairs. Graffiti identified the gangs claiming and competing for the tenement as territory. At the first-floor door, Rivera peered into the lobby before stepping out.

He saw the clerk staring at a television behind the steel wire and bulletproof glass of the manager's office. An elderly resident of the deteriorating hotel slept in an overstuffed chair salvaged from some garbage heap. A Mexican resident pushed through the doors. Recognizing the Mexican as an illegal, Rivera knew he could leave the hotel without risking walking into a squad of Immigration and Naturalization officers.

With a quick *"Buenos"* to the Mexican, Rivera hurried out. Derelicts and winos sprawled on the sidewalk, warming themselves in the late-afternoon sunlight. Rush-hour traffic from the offices of downtown Los Angeles sped past. With their windows rolled up, secretaries and lawyers and accountants drove past without looking at the human dregs littering Main Street.

Rivera hurried to the corner of Eighth and Main. There, he went to a pay phone in the corner of a café. Taking a business card from his wallet, he punched the buttons for a San Francisco number. After depositing a dollar in coins, the phone rang.

"Good evening, Holt, Lindsey and Stein."

"*Buenas tardes*. May I speak with Mr. Holt."

"This is the answering service, sir. The office is closed for the day. Would you like to leave a message, sir?"

"Mr. Holt has gone home?"

"I have no idea, sir. I only take messages for the office."

"This is Antonio Rivera calling—" He turned the card over. On the back, David Holt had written his home number. "I will call Mr. Holt's home. I must speak with him personally. Thank you."

"Good night, Mr. Rivera."

The second call cost him the last of his coins. After several rings, a young man answered the phone.

"This is the Holt residence. Who is calling?"

"*Buenas tardes*. This is Antonio Rivera. May I please speak with Mr. Holt?"

Only a quick intake of breath answered him. He heard a hand close over the phone. Then the voice returned.

"Mr. Rivera, this is Michael Holt. My father's dead."

A cold fear seized Rivera. Though he dreaded what he must ask, he asked nevertheless, his mouth dry, "An accident?"

"No, sir. He was murdered."

"Who...?"

"We don't know who. But it's important for you to help us now. My father talked of your case. He was on his way to the airport to go to Washington, when they kidnapped him—''

"Los escuadrones de muerte . . . aquí."

"What, sir?"

"The death squads. Here."

"Floyd Jefferson went to your apartment in San Diego. But your family was gone. We were afraid that—"

"We saw the Immigration. So we left."

"Can we have your new address, please? We need your help. The police won't believe why this happened."

"North Americans don't understand. They killed my son and the North Americans said it was the Communists. They killed Señor Marquez and . . . ."

"Will you talk with the police, Mr. Rivera?"

"If they send us back to El Salvador, we all die. I, my wife, my daughters. *Los escuadrones* wait for us."

"You will not be deported. You are now material witnesses in a murder investigation. An American murder investigation. My father's law firm will bring you to San Francisco. We will protect you. If you have any difficulties with the officials, we make bail for your entire family. We need your help. . . . Please, we need your address and phone number."

"I have no telephone. We stay at a hotel in Los Angeles—'' Rivera gave Michael Holt the name and address of the Main Street tenement.

"Thank you, Mr. Rivera. Together perhaps we can bring my father's and your son's murderers to justice. Tomorrow, a friend of my father will go to Los Angeles. I'll call him now. He's the personal aide to a congressman. He's offered to help us in every way possible.''

"I'm am so very, very sorry my troubles have killed your father.''

"No, not your troubles. Our troubles. Now we are together in this....''

"What is his name? This man who will come for my family?''

"Robert Prescott.''

25

A night wind from the Atlantic misted the lush tropical garden. Lights hidden among the flowers—transplanted from Salvador—created shadows and translucent colors. Colonel Roberto Quesada walked the cobblestoned paths of his estate. Though he appeared calm and impassive to the trusted guards stationed at the corners of his property, the colonel's mind raged with anger and impotence. His hands knotted into fists inside the deep pockets of his silk smoking robe. Quesada stared furiously at the lights of Miami.

He cursed his allegiance with the North Americans. The weaklings, incompetent weaklings. But what could he expect of men who would betray their country for Salvadoran gold?

Often, his disgust at his allegiance with the gringos threatened to shatter the mask of diplomacy he maintained. He gave them *abrazos* of brotherly friendship. He called them his allies in the war against international communism. He contributed hundreds of thousands of dollars to their political campaigns.

But they would never have the strength and discipline required for victory. Quesada saw it in their faces. Once, when he made the mistake of including a gringo politician—a Republican who claimed to support the principles of private property and military strength—in a breakfast conversation, an officer joked about "cleaning out the lice" that had populated a region Quesada needed for the production of coffee. The Republican asked why "lice eradication" involved the army. Did the Salvadoran army supervise the use of insecticides? The officers gathered around the breakfast table had laughed. "Only for the eradication of Indian lice." But the Republican went white when he realized the officer had directed the killing of thousands of Indian *campesinos*.

How the North American had degenerated in only a hundred years! Quesada had read the history of North America. All of North America had been the land of the Indians. The European settlers had marched west over the bones of Indians. Their generals had stated: "The only good Indian is a dead Indian." "From nits come lice."

Now, as El Salvador attempted to maintain the purity of its Spanish heritage and culture against the Indian and *mestizo* Communists, the North Americans talked of land reform, of law, of justice

Of human rights.

What rights? Perhaps men and women did have rights. But the racially impure? The sickening halfbreeds of lustful soldiers and Indian whores? The slothful poor in their filthy slums? The ignorant? The masses of *campesinos* who spoke their subhuman dialects, their supposed language an affront and slander to the melodious mother tongue of Castile?

The Communists recruited those filthy slum creatures for their wars against the Families. Scum led scum.

But why did the North Americans take their cause also? White people marched in "solidarity with the people of El Salvador." To protest military aid, the educated and prosperous North Americans poured their own blood on the steps of federal offices. Although inflation and unemployment racked their country, North Americans sent medicine, food, clothing, and United States dollars to the revolutionaries.

Only an international communist conspiracy explained the strange phenomenon. Jews and Communists and dreamers funneled their propaganda into the empty minds of North Americans.

The major newspapers of North America—all Communist controlled. The radio and television networks—Communist controlled. The publishers—Communists.

Worse, the elected officials of the United States now mouthed Communist lies.

Land reform.

Elections.

Justice.

What nonsense! Where would the land for the Communists come from? The Families had developed the lands throughout the centuries since their Spanish forefathers brought civilization to El Salvador. Why should the Families give up ancestral holdings? And elections, another joke. Allow the ignorant and poor and subhuman to vote? What would they vote for except the theft of land and wealth? And justice. Prosecute soldiers for killing Communists? Nonsense!

Colonel Quesada had launched the war against the

North American Communists to combat the lies threatening the survival of his nation. Victory in El Salvador would not guarantee the future of the Families. Not while North Americans continued their assaults on El Salvador's traditions and culture.

A few North Americans volunteered to join Quesada in his war against the contagion in the English-speaking Americas. Others accepted his gold. All of his North American allies recognized the historical imperative to destroy the nonwhite insurgents, whether they fought in Sonsonate Province or Liberty City.

But their decision to fight did not mean they had the strength and discipline.

Or the will to act as necessary.

Robert Prescott had failed him. When he had the opportunity to kill the black journalist, he did not. The congressional aide had talked with the journalist throughout the night, but had not killed him. Prescott had instead hired two local gunmen. The gunmen failed. Then Prescott had hired black nationalist mercenaries to pursue the journalist and his three guards. Again Prescott's hired gunmen failed.

Now California newspapers carried photos of dead men on the freeway.

Not only had Prescott failed to execute the Communist, he had failed to inform Quesada of the true threat presented by the "three specialists from Washington." He had failed to tell Quesada the three men carried military weapons.

When Quesada dispatched Captain Madrano to intercept the reporter and his three guards, the Salvadorans died in an ambush. True, Captain Madrano should have recognized the trap, but without proper information, any man might have blundered into the ambush.

Furthermore, how could he possibly discipline Madrano, the son of Quesada's lifelong friend and business partner?

Agent Gallucci confirmed the military weapons and precise tactics the "specialists" employed. Perhaps Madrano could be forgiven his defeat.

Fortunately, Gallucci eliminated the coward in the hospital, who had survived the defeat, before he could betray his commander and his fatherland to the North American media. Of all the North Americans, only Gallucci had demonstrated any ability. As he should. His loyalty cost more than any of the other hired gringos.

But Gallucci had not found the Riveras. Nor could Gallucci eliminate the black Communist journalist while the specialists protected him.

Now the defeat of Captain Madrano's squad forced Colonel Quesada to commit another squad of soldiers to the pursuit of the reporter. The young officer, the son of his dear friend, would have another chance to execute the Communists.

First, the journalist. Then the Communist traitor Rivera. Quesada had given orders that Rivera not die before he had seen his children suffer. The tortures Captain Madrano was going to inflict on the children would be punishment for Rivera's treason.

But how to remove the "specialists" who interfered with Quesada's justice?

Prescott had told Quesada that the "specialists"

had come from Washington after a request by Congressman Buckley—that foul male whore whom the degenerates and blacks and socialists of San Francisco had elected to serve the interests of debauchery and Soviet Russia. Obviously, *puto* Buckley had friends in Washington.

Colonel Quesada also had friends in Washington. He had hesitated to request their help, but now he must. His friends shared his resolve to defeat the sub-human Communist scum and all their sympathizers. Yet Quesada doubted their resolve. They had never fought a war like Quesada fought. They thought of wars as confrontations of armies on the field of battle, of tanks and airplanes and artillery striking at the enemy until the enemy surrendered.

El Salvador fought a different war. Quesada had heard many North Americans discuss the realities of his nation's struggles, but only the Americans who belonged to very conservative political parties actually understood.

The Nazi Party of the United States understood. As Quesada entered his luxurious home, he realized he faced a long, long struggle. He must reform the politics of North America through education and armed struggle. Teach the wealthy the reality of a political war. Then make war against those who would steal the wealth of the elite.

Without vigilance and unrelenting war against the subversives, private property and economic freedom would never be secure.

All sources of subversion—Indians, blacks, Asians, Jews, eastern-European immigrants, intellectuals, unions, Protestants, "born-again Christians," reformist Catholics—must be exterminated. Only then could the United States be a strong ally of El Salvador.

Without the extermination of the subversives, no one of high birth or privilege would be safe.

Quesada went to his study, where he could speak without any of his soldiers or family overhearing him. As he unlocked his book of names and phone numbers, the telephone rang.

"Buenas noches."

"Hello, Colonel?" Robert Prescott asked, his voice urgent.

The colonel could not restrain his anger. "Do you know what has happened? Do you know how many men died because of your incompetence?"

But the North American's words calmed the enraged colonel.

"I know where the Riveras are," Prescott said.

26

As the last light of the western horizon faded to the turquoise of night, Able Team parked on one of the boulevards near Los Angeles International Airport. Down the block, a neon sign advertised full-size Fords at economy rates. They had abandoned the Silverado in Monterey, rented a Chevrolet from a tourist agency, driven that car to Los Angeles. Now they intended to rent another car. No one would follow their trail to San Diego.

Blancanales glanced at his watch. "Time to check in with Stony Man. If we wait until we get to San Diego it'll be one in the morning back east."

"And I'll need to make calls," Lyons told them. "I've got police friends in San Diego. Maybe we can get some liaison for the search there—"

"Maybe we won't need any help," Jefferson interrupted. "Hold off on the calls to San Diego until I call San Francisco. The Riveras had Mr. Holt's office and home numbers. If they're okay, they'll call him."

"He gave out his home phone number?" Lyons asked with surprise. "Doesn't sound like any lawyer I ever met."

"Mr. Holt knew they needed him. That's the kind of guy he was. I guess I'll call his family, ask if they got news."

Gadgets stayed in the rented car as the others went to a row of pay phones behind the gas station. He sprawled out in the front seat, his sneakers on the steering wheel, his head against the passenger door. By habit, he adjusted the rearview mirror so he could watch behind him without moving. He always called Lyons "paranoid," but in fact, they all qualified as paranoids.

You deal with snakes, you learn to be a snake charmer.

Like that Holt lawyer. He knew he had taken on a case involving terrorism. Right-wing Salvadoran terrorism, but still the same: terrorism. And the case ate at him.

Gadgets wondered if they really faced right-wingers. *This is all too weird.* What would the Salvadorans have to gain by wasting North Americans? Only made for headlines.

And the headlines made Congress scream. After those four missionaries got snuffed, Gadgets had figured the job for a Commie hit. Why not? What is worse than murdering nuns?

Raping nuns, then offing them, that's what. If a newsman had interviewed Gadgets Schwarz—ex-Green Beret and expert on Vietnamese Stalinist terrorism—he would have said the Commies had dressed up in government uniforms and offed the women. The People's Army of Vietnam specialized in crazy numbers like that. Dress up in South Vietnamese uniforms and walk through a village shooting little kids. Or get some rice in bags that bore the stencil of an American flag and mix in some poison. Or send in one sniper to kill a few Americans in a passing patrol so they would call down an airstrike on the village.

That was the way Commies operated. But then on national television, what does he see? Salvadoran soldiers confessing to the murders. Too much. Nothing like murdering Americans with American weapons to make Americans think twice about sending more weapons and ammunition.

Then those two labor lawyers. Wow. Zap someone in the local Sheraton coffee shop and think no one will notice? What did the Salvadorans expect people in the United States to think? Maybe the lawyers didn't tip and a waiter got pissed? So he put a few bursts of .45 ACP through them?

Then all the others. The tourist who got shot "while attempting to escape." Except that he had powder burns on the back of his head. The Dutch newsmen who got caught in a "cross fire" and took point-blank bursts. What does that mean, cross fire in a phone booth?

And this Ricardo Marquez, the reporter. Hack off his head and leave it on a fence post? Even the PAVN wouldn't do that to a reporter. Makes for piss-poor press relations.

If he did not know the facts, if he did not know for a fact that Cubans and Nicaraguans actually did fight in the mountains with the rebels, Gadgets would have suspected the Salvadoran government was a Communist plot.

Forty thousand death-squad murders in three years! Thinking about that made his gut twist. Forget the Cubans and Nicaraguans and the Commies; if Gadgets

Schwarz was a Salvadoran, he would be in the mountains, too. After he put down the death squads, he would fight it out with the Commies.

He saw Blancanales and Lyons jog back to the car. The expressions on their faces told him something had gone wrong. Blancanales jerked open the door.

"They've canceled the mission."

"What?"

Lyons got in the back seat as Blancanales explained. "Washington has downgraded this to witness protection. They told Brognola the FBI will take it over in the morning."

"What do you make of that?" Lyons sneered. "I don't think I'd feel very safe with a collection of overweight bureau boys packing thirty-eights, up against Salvadoran Nazis and the Black Liberation Army."

Gadgets blinked. "What? Black Liberation Army?"

Blancanales nodded. "That's who tried to hit us on 101 South. One of their wounded said a white man hired them to hit some CIA spooks. That's us. The white man paid in Krugerrands."

"Bet you one of those Krugerrands," Lyons hissed, "that the white man was Prescott."

Looking at Lyons's face, Gadgets laughed. "I think I just heard someone pronounce a sentence of death. Not subject to the approval of the Supreme Court."

"Speaking of a death sentence," Blancanales continued, "that Salvadoran we left at the hospital? He's dead."

"He should have made it!" Gadgets said. "You had him stabilized. He just needed a cast and a transfusion."

"After he left the recovery ward, someone smothered him."

Lyons shook his head. "Those Salvadorans. . . ."

They all turned at once as they heard Jefferson's shoes slap the asphalt. The young man sprinted to the car. In the streetlight, they saw his face as white as his gold-toned skin would allow. He gasped out the words.

"The Riveras called the Holts. They're in Los Angeles. And the Holts sent Bob Prescott to pick them up. He knows where they are!"

The men of Able Team looked at one another. Stony Man had canceled their mission. The Federal Bureau of Investigation now had the case. If Able Team went to the aid of the Rivera family, they violated their authorization.

But their eyes voted to help the Riveras.

Blancanales spoke first. "Our man in Washington told us the FBI would take it over in the morning—"

"Not the FBI!" Jefferson startled at the mention of the bureau. "Holt trusted the FBI and now... now. . . ."

Blancanales calmed the young reporter with a hand on his shoulder. "Just because they told us we're off the case, doesn't mean we'll get off it."

Floyd Jefferson looked at the three "specialists" he had learned to respect and trust. "You'll help the Riveras? Even if it's not your job anymore?"

"I'm free," Lyons joked. He questioned his partners: "You guys got something else you'd rather do?"

27

Cruising past the neon-bright bars and porno theaters of Main Street, Able Team scanned the few parked cars and trucks. Derelicts sprawled beneath the blue white glare of streetlights. Others gathered in doorways or shuffled through the alleys, shadows within the skid-row desolation. Beyond the two- or three-story shops and hotels dating from the 1930s, the light patterns of the contemporary Los Angeles high-rise skyline stood against the night like an image from a dream.

Here, where alcohol and 16mm pornography had replaced hope for crowds of Americans born in the United States, other Americans—speaking Mexican-Spanish and Quechua and the patois of Belize—hoped for a life in a country free of institutionalized poverty and racism. Often, after weeks of bus travel through Central America and Mexico, then days of claustrophobic transportation in the closed trucks and vans of smugglers, the immigrants' first vision of the United States shocked them: to see the filth of Main Street, to see the gaunt winos wandering in search of intoxication, to see and hear the raving street-crazies—the immigrants feared they had journeyed thousands of miles only to join the inmates of a vast prison.

But when they searched for work, they saw the other

sections of Los Angeles. Men returned to their families in the hotels and told of neighborhoods where the decent Americans lived.

Though they described the mansions of the superrich on Sunset Boulevard and the fabulous wealth of the shopping centers, the other neighborhoods gave them the strength to return to their menial jobs every morning. The streets of the small houses, with the battered cars and work trucks parked in the driveways, gave them hope. A man who worked with his hands could never hope to join the rich. But he could hope for the chance of a steady job, then an apartment, then—after a decade of working six or seven days a week plus overtime—a house and a place in a community of free Americans.

The men and women from the villages knew the United States offered them the hope of self-improvement. If they stayed in their villages, they could expect only poverty and disease and early death, but in the north. . . .

If a man and woman worked, they could buy a car, they could go to night school, they could send their children to school, they could buy medicine so most of their children lived. They could hope.

Only hope and faith sustained the immigrants thrown into the cesspool of Main Street. They feared any contact with the authorities of the United States. Rather than risk questions as to their immigration status, crimes went unreported, children went hungry, diseases went untreated. The honest, struggling immigrants enjoyed none of the services the derelicts and winos exploited. The immigrants feared the Immigration and Naturalization Service more than hunger, disease or robbery. The INS could end their dreams with handcuffs and deportation.

Lyons knew every doorway and alley, every step of Main Street. As a rookie with the Los Angeles Police Department, he had walked the downtown streets with his regulation uniform and weapons, utterly confused and frustrated by what he encountered. If the department's regulations had also required that he speak the languages of the people he encountered, he might have helped them. Instead, he often saw bloody victims run from him. He heard conversations stop when he appeared. He saw murderers drinking and laughing because witnesses to their crimes would not speak to a detective.

Once, a Spanish-speaking officer had typed a card for him. In Spanish, the card stated that the police department did not work for Immigration. It stated that Patrolman Lyons would never betray anyone to Immigration. That they could trust the Anglo.

But many of the illegals could not read. Literate *campesinos* presented an unacceptable threat to aristocracies and military governments; therefore, schools did not exist in the villages and slums of Latin America. The card became only one more frustration for the rookie cop.

Even after reassignment and promotions, Lyons often returned to central Los Angeles to hunt the predators hiding in the tenements and alleys. But then he knew to bring a Spanish-speaking officer. Ironically, Lyons regretted that expediency; if he had learned the language himself, he would be a more valuable warrior now.

Passing the tenement where the Riveras hid, Gadgets wheeled the rented car around the block. On Spring Street, Lyons turned to Blancanales.

"You and Jefferson go in the hotel. I'll cover the back on foot. Wizard, park in front. Keep the engine running. Looks like we beat the goons, but who knows?"

"The Riveras know," Blancanales answered.

"True." Lyons nodded as he assembled his equipment. He clipped his hand-radio to his belt. Dropping two speedloaders for his Colt Python into his jacket's left pocket, he took a second pistol from his suitcase.

Unlike his partners, he did not carry a Beretta 93-R. The silenced Italian pistol required a perfect head shot for an instant kill. Underpowered to avoid the crack of the bullets breaking the speed of sound, the slugs had many times failed to knock down the enraged, adrenaline-charged men Lyons had faced. Konzaki, the Stony Man weaponsmith, had hand-crafted a hybrid auto-pistol for Lyons, stealing the best features of the Berettas—the selective-fire auto-sear, the oversize trigger guard and fold-down left-hand lever that provided a two-handed grip. The bastardized Colt Government Model pistol had proved itself on two missions, the first in Cairo, the second in Guatemala.

"Colt Frankenstein," Gadgets joked.

Lyons laughed as he shoved the silenced auto-pistol under his belt at the small of his back.

"You can tell he's serious," Gadgets continued, " 'cause that thing is dangerous."

An extra ten-round magazine of .45 ACP hollow-points went in Lyons's wallet pocket. He gave his partners a wave as he left the car. "See you guys later."

As Lyons disappeared into the shadows of an alley, Gadgets made another right turn. Blancanales snapped back the slide on his Beretta 93-R. He eased down the hammer. The double-action pistol had a heavy trigger pull, but Blancanales did not believe the situation warranted carrying the pistol cocked and locked. He heard paper rustle as Jefferson concealed his shortened Smith & Wesson and a box of shells in a shopping bag.

"You got a round in the chamber?" he asked the young reporter.

Jefferson nodded. "You better believe it."

"It isn't safe. Unload."

"We could be walking into a goon squad. It isn't safe *not* to be loaded."

"You're going into a hotel crowded with people. Little kids. You want to chance an accident? That thing will take a child's legs *off*. You want to live with that? Dream about it the rest of your life?"

The young man looked down at the short-barreled weapon that had already saved his life twice. Blancanales saw indecision and fear on his face. Both men—the ex-Green Beret and the free-lance writer—knew what they faced if the Salvadorans took them alive. And what the Riveras faced if the Salvadorans took the family.

"Wait. I've got a compromise," Blancanales told him. "First, those shells, put them in your pockets. Then clear the chamber, reload, but don't close the bolt. Keep it slightly open. And when we walk in there, you keep your right hand in the bag, on the weapon.

Something happens, snap the slide forward with your left hand and your right hand's already on the action. No feeling for the safety. It's called 'Unlocked Carry.'"

"Yeah, makes sense."

As Jefferson readied his weapon, Gadgets and Blancanales gave Main Street a last scan. Then Blancanales ducked his head low and spoke into his hand-radio.

"Ironman, where are you?"

"Looking down on you," Lyons answered.

"That was quick."

"When you going in?"

"Right now. Over and out."

Parking illegally, Gadgets stopped the rented car. Blancanales and Jefferson crossed the sidewalk and pushed through the doors. Gadgets pulled away. He continued to the far end of the block and parked, the engine running.

The lobby stank of mildew and stale tobacco. Blancanales saw the clerk sleeping with his head on the desk. Three haggard residents shared a gallon bottle of wine. They watched the two visitors pass. Blancanales kept his face turned away.

At the stairway, Blancanales paused an instant. He listened. Then he jerked the fire door open but did not step into the stairwell. He snapped a glance into a brightly lit landing. No one. They went up the stairs quickly, almost silently, their soft-soled shoes making no sound. But the old stairs creaked.

They paused again at the second-floor stairwell. Blancanales motioned Jefferson to continue up the stairs, whispered: "Make some noise...."

Jefferson's scuffs and footsteps broke the silence of the stairwell. Blancanales counted sixty and jerked the door open. Snapping his head out, then back, he saw no one in the corridor. He hissed for Jefferson to return.

In the corridor, they heard televisions and voices. A woman berated someone in Georgia-accented English. Jefferson glanced at a room number, then pointed to a door. The moldy carpeting silenced their steps.

Blancanales went flat against the wall as Jefferson knocked. "Señor Rivera...*estoy aqui*...Floyd. Floyd Jefferson. *¿Recuerdeme usted? El niño del arco iris.*"

Silence for a moment, then laughter behind the door. It eased open. Señor Rivera called out, "Is there anyone with you?"

"Yes, I have a friend with me. His name is Rosario." Jefferson motioned for Blancanales to show himself.

"Bienviendo, amigos." Señor Rivera opened the door wide for his visitors.

As he entered, Blancanales glanced behind the door out of force of habit. A middle-aged Salvadoran woman—Señora Rivera—stood there with a butcher knife, raised to stab. He slowly lifted his left hand, palm open. Rivera tut-tutted his wife. *"Todo es bueno ahora,"* he told her. He apologized to Blancanales and Jefferson as he shook hands. "One cannot be too careful in difficult times."

"And these are very difficult times," Blancanales agreed. "Señor Rivera, allow me to express my sorrow for the death of your son."

"Thank you for your compassion."

Blancanales keyed his hand-radio. "We're here. The family's okay. Wizard, how's the street look?"

"No Prescott yet."

Lyons's voice answered also. "He is one man I am watching for, no doubt about it."

"Relax. We might be here until morning. Over."

Señora Rivera motioned for them to sit. Only folding chairs and a mattress furnished the room. The three daughters watched the strangers from the mattress, a single blanket pulled around their shoulders. A portable television sat on the windowsill. A wooden packing crate served as both a table and a stand for an electric coil.

"Coffee?" the Señora offered.

"Gracias," Blancanales accepted. "It will be a long night."

"We are ready to go to San Francisco." Rivera gestured at the furnishings of the room and laughed. "We can pack in two minutes."

"Not tonight," Blancanales said. "Maybe tomorrow or the next day."

"But Michael Holt, Mr. Holt's son, said he would send Mr. Robert Prescott to take us to San Francisco. He said perhaps tonight. Certainly tomorrow."

Blancanales shook his head, no. Then he explained what must be done.

28

Only minutes after his arrival at Los Angeles International Airport, Robert Prescott parked in the garage of the Sheraton Hotel. As he locked the rented car, his eyes searched the shadows and unnatural fluorescent glare of the stark cavern of structural concrete and gleaming automobiles. He saw no one watching from the other vehicles. No one loitered near the elevators. He did see a panel van—like the vans favored by surveillance teams—but a concrete pillar blocked the view from its front windows. The back windows faced away from him.

As he headed for the elevators, the roar of a late-night flight drowned out the sound of his feet on the pavement. He tried to keep his eyes straight ahead, to watch around him for surveillance only with his peripheral vision, but his fear forced him to keep turning his head for surreptitious glances.

The operation had gone public. West Coast and national newscasts carried the stories and video images of the death squad Prescott had hired to kill "a leading black reporter and his heavily armed goon guards." Though the commentators lacked the imagination or paranoia to link the killings of Salvadorans and ex-con assassins in San Francisco with the freeway battle, the late-breaking and fragmentary reports of the ambush slayings of the "illegal Mexicans" in the mountains outside of San Jose would hit the headlines tomorrow.

Finally the commentators would connect the several incidents. The weapons used to kill the ex-cons and black nationalists would link the cases.

Though he had been careful, though he had handled the negotiations, the assignments and the payments without meetings, Prescott feared the relentless probing of an investigation of any sort. If the news media interviewed a hundred ex-cons, militants and extremists, one of them might remember the bright young lawyer who always offered legal advice and loaned money.

Years before, as an idealistic law student volunteering legal services to prisoners and paroled felons, he had gained entry to an underground society of dope dealers and murderers.

Later, after joining the congressman's circle of advisors, he learned the role of more sophisticated criminals in politics. The chic radicals of the jet set—San Francisco socialists, Manhattan Marxists, the corrupt elite of the capital—depended on heroin and cocaine and Quaaludes for euphoria and erotic novelty. Organized crime supplied the radical Left with the drugs. Soon, gang leaders appeared at fund-raisers, at first for the amusement of watching cocaine-dazed politicians attempt to explain international policy, later to sink their teeth into the elite who drafted the laws and appointed the prosecutors.

The gangsters had always contributed money to both conservatives and liberals, but they saw their future in the liberals. The people of the United States resisted the severe limitations of responsible fiscal policy. The liberals promised everything to everyone. Organized crime knew who would win the next election. Gang leaders became the Left's strongest supporters.

Prescott exploited his encounters with the gangsters. He offered them assassins unknown to the criminal hierarchies or federal investigators. Need a Mafia lawyer silenced before he testified to a grand jury in New York? Fly in a black ex-con to stage a parking-lot mugging and killing. Then fly the murderer on to Libya to live a life of luxury with the security of monthly payments from a numbered Swiss account. The felon did not know whom he killed. Unless he returned to the United States and searched library news files, the murderer would never know. But if he returned, he lost his payments and his luxuries. And his life.

As the administration increased the flow of North American wealth to the Salvadoran war, Prescott made contact with the Fascists sheltered in Miami. He offered them a twofold service: assassins and information. If necessary, North American felons and psychopaths would murder Salvadoran refugees. If necessary, they would murder others, people more conspicuous, people who were in the public eye and were hated by the public: the assassins would murder incurably recidivist child molesters, activist personalities, radical and criminal celebrities, anyone whose death would earn the killers the public's silent thanks, and thus help cover up the true origins of the crimes against the refugees.

As a leftist lawyer assisting a liberal congress-man, Prescott received a warm welcome to the homes and offices of expatriate Salvadorans. He report-ed their words and thoughts to the Salvadoran fas-cists.

But he regretted the day he took their Krugerrands. Dead Salvadorans meant nothing to him. The murder of North Americans, however, was a different matter. The cover of vigilantism could barely protect him from the repulsion that would strike when each kill was broadcast.

Now, as he pressed the elevator button for the upper floors of the Sheraton, his body quivered with fear. When the elevator stopped at the lobby, Prescott ex-pected Federal Bureau of Investigation officers to step in and seize him. Instead, four drunken tourists in party hats stumbled inside, continued their disco danc-ing.

As the elevator doors slid open on the sixth floor, Prescott shoved past the tourists. His imagination put federal agents behind every door. They waited for him at every corner in the corridor.

Striding toward the room where Captain Madrano waited, Prescott saw a Hispanic bellboy pushing a cart of dirty dishes and beer bottles. A federal agent? Pres-cott turned his back to the young man. Fumbling in his pocket, Prescott pretended to be searching for his room key. When the bellboy wheeled the cart around a corner, Prescott broke into a run. He beat on Captain Madrano's door.

"*¿Quién está allá?*"

Prescott's fear would not allow him to say his name

out loud. But he would speak the Salvadoran's name for the hidden microphones. "Madrano?"

A man spoke in Spanish, then the laughter of several men exploded inside. The door opened. Captain Madrano received Prescott with a sneering smile. Dapper in tailored slacks, a Ralph Lauren tapered shirt and a black leather shoulder holster carrying a Beretta, the ORDEN officer sipped at a tumbler of bourbon.

Ten other Salvadorans watched the North American traitor enter. In front of them, open suitcases exposed Uzi submachine guns. The Salvadorans looked at the nervous, sweating lawyer, then returned to their bourbon and magazine loading. A wooden case of PMC 9mm cartridges lay on a coffee table. Most of the men loaded Uzi mags. One man inventoried the contents of another suitcase.

Glancing into the cluttered suitcase, Prescott could not identify the objects.

"So. You are ready?" Captain Madrano demanded of the North American.

"Isn't it dangerous to meet here?" Prescott asked, hearing his voice quaver. "Someone could see us. A policeman. A bellboy. A clerk. Anyone."

Captain Madrano turned to his men. *"El puto norteamericano piensa que un hotel Sheraton es peligroso."* The other men laughed at what the captain had said. He turned back to Prescott. "Of all places, it is secure here."

"Where do I take them?" Prescott asked.

A man brought him a map of Los Angeles. Red ink marked a location in Lennox. Prescott recognized the area where the State of California Department of

Transportation had planned the Century Freeway, condemning and purchasing thousands of homes, then canceling the project due to the onslaught of environmentalists and OPEC gasoline prices. The strip of abandoned neighborhoods had become a wasteland of vandalized and burned homes, a no-man's-land where street gangs fought wars, and sexual psychopaths took kidnapped young girls for orgies of sadistic sex. Prescott realized the Salvadorans employed other Californians. No tourist book or city map touted that slash of desolation.

"From Main Street," Captain Madrano instructed, "you will go south on the Harbor Freeway, to Century Boulevard. They will not suspect. Even if they have a map, they will see the jet planes in the sky. If they question you, say you are not familiar with Los Angeles. Here, you will make a wrong turn. You will say you made a wrong turn, then you make more wrong turns. We will wait."

"What if I actually do get lost?"

"We have thought of that. Here." The captain gave Prescott a small walkie-talkie. "Put it in your coat. If you have a problem, you can switch on the radio, like this. Then talk of the problem. Say, 'This street, that street.' Stop and examine your map. We will come and take them. But I tell you, there will be no problem. You will be done with this very quickly. But they will not...."

As the young Salvadoran officer ended his instructions with a laugh, the man searching through the cluttered suitcase also laughed. The man took something out of the interior.

"Three girls and a mother?" the man asked.

"*Sí.*" The captain nodded.

Prescott saw what the man held. Four waterproof highway flares. The man smiled, then sang as he set the flares aside: "Your love is burning, burning, a fire deep inside me, burning, burning. . . ."

The image of what the Salvadorans intended struck Prescott. He staggered back, fell against the door, his mind spinning, vomit acid in his throat. Captain Madrano and the other ORDEN soldiers laughed. Madrano dismissed Prescott with a sneer.

"Go. We expect you within an hour. If you fail us, we take you. Understand, gringo?"

Nodding, Prescott fumbled for the knob. He fell out the door. He put one hand against the corridor wall, breathed deeply for a moment. He sought comfort in the sterile decor and computer-determined colors of the Sheraton corridor. When his panic and nausea faded, he stumbled to the elevators.

Arrest by federal agents no longer panicked him. The thought of prison no longer made his body shiver. Now he thought of prison as a sanctuary.

As the elevator dropped silently to the garages, Prescott closed his eyes. He focused on the nothingness behind his eyelids, hoping the darkness would bring peace.

But he only saw an image from one of the shocking films smuggled out of El Salvador: the shattered skull of a young woman, the machete-carved flesh of her face curling back from the long wounds, her eyes swarming with flies.

Even when his eyes snapped open, even when he

stared at the chrome floor-indicator flashing with the back-lit plastic numbers, he could not help but zoom in on that girl's shattered skull, the blood-clotted matted hair tangled around a vast bullet exit wound. Like the camera, his mind zoomed in to focus on the secret of El Salvador: A human brain feeding a squirming mass of translucent worms.

Now Prescott truly understood the men who paid him Krugerrand gold.

29

In the room, Captain Madrano spoke into a walkie-talkie. "He has left. Can you hear him?"

FBI Agent Gallucci watched Prescott stagger from the elevator. The San Francisco lawyer fell to his hands and knees on the garage floor and vomited. The minitransmitter built into the walkie-talkie that Prescott carried sent every breath and gasp to the receiver in Gallucci's ear.

"I can hear him, I can see him. What did you give him to drink?"

"I would not drink with him."

"He's puking."

"*Con miedo.*" Captain Madrano laughed.

"What's he got to be afraid of?"

"Us, if he fails."

Gallucci laughed also. "He's going to his car. It's a blue Dodge. A rented one. In case he does screw up, you got some men who can find their way around Los Angeles?"

"Of course. One of my lieutenants went to UCLA."

"It won't be good, but those illegals have got to go. Tell your men to do it fast and get out. Main Street has a one-minute response time, once the police switchboard gets a call. If anyone bothers to call. There he goes. On my way.''

"I see you later.''

"You bet on it. One of the girls is a teenager, right?''

"Thirteen years or fourteen. A Communist beauty.''

"I won't miss the party. Over and out, amigo.''

Starting his unmarked agency car, Gallucci eased out of his parking place. He accelerated into traffic, following the taillights of Prescott's rented car. Gallucci realized the car looked much like his own, a solid gray Dodge four-door. Only the colors differed.

Now I know where the bureau gets these dogs, they buy them used from rental companies. But I won't have to drive these used-up wrecks next year. Take an early retirement, pack up my bag of Salvadoran gold, move someplace where the living is easy. And the peasants obedient. And the little girls hot for dollars. If Quesada and his boys deal with the revolution, El Salvador would be great. If not, I'll go where they go. . . .

Gallucci had no problem following the blue Dodge. Prescott followed the San Diego Freeway north to the Santa Monica Freeway, then went east to the civic center. The late-night traffic screened Gallucci from Prescott's rearview mirror.

The sounds Gallucci was monitoring indicated that Prescott had taken the threat from Captain Madrano really seriously. The minitransmitter sent the sounds of the lawyer mumbling to himself, of dry heaves and of choked sobs.

Yep, they definitely put the fear of God into that jerk.

When Prescott left the Santa Monica Freeway and

went north through the deserted manufacturing and retail areas, Gallucci veered off to a parallel street.

He sped to Main Street and parked a block and a half north of the hotel. The square cargo van compartment of a produce truck concealed most of his bureau Dodge.

Looking diagonally across the four empty lanes of Main Street, Gallucci watched as Prescott parked his rented Dodge. The minimike in the lawyer's coat pocket transmitted every sound to Gallucci's receiver. The stark glare of a mercury-arc street lamp lit the entry to the hotel like a spotlight.

Gallucci watched and listened as Prescott slammed his car door. But then the audio went silent.

Damn that jerk! Gallucci cursed as Prescott crossed the sidewalk. The frightened lawyer, for whatever reason, had left the walkie-talkie and its concealed minitransmitter in the Dodge.

But Gallucci had an excellent view of the hotel. Prescott could not leave unobserved.

The moonlighting FBI agent waited, watched.

30

Throwing Prescott down, Blancanales put his knee in the screaming man's back. He forced Prescott's face into the filthy carpet to silence him. Señor Rivera grabbed their prisoner's hands. Jefferson checked the hallway for *Blancos*, then pulled the door closed and locked it.

"None out there," Jefferson told them.

Señora Rivera huddled on the mattress with her daughters. She held the girls' heads against her bosom so they would not see what the men did. The eight-year-old turned to peek at the scene of brutality and terror. Lidia pulled the blanket over her daughter's face.

"Where is the death squad waiting?" Blancanales asked Prescott.

"What? What do you mean?" gasped Prescott at the carpet. "What are you doing to me? Are you a law officer? Do you know that you are violating every police procedure and every civil right—"

Blancanales shoved Prescott's face into the carpet again. Keying his hand-radio, he reported to his partners, "I have him. What do you see out there?"

"Nada," Gadgets answered. "Unless you mean boozer losers."

"No one else got out of the car," Lyons reported. "Looks like he's alone."

"Any other cars?"

"Not on this block," Lyons answered.

"No goon squads," Gadgets reported.

"Wizard," Lyons spoke again. "Watch the front. I'm going to the back. Pol, is he talking?"

"Not yet."

"If he won't, let me know."

"Will do." Blancanales returned his hand-radio to his coat pocket. He knotted his fingers in the styled hair of the lawyer and pulled his head back.

"Where are the *Blancos*?"

"This is assault, false arrest, false imprisonment—"

Bearing down his knee, Blancanales pulled Prescott's head back until he felt the vertebra creak. The lawyer gasped and choked. His voice low and smooth, Blancanales asked again:

"Where are the *Blancos*?"

Prescott struggled against their hold on him, kicking his legs, straining to twist his head free. Blancanales and Señor Rivera held firm until Prescott broke into sobs. Blancanales took plastic handcuffs out of his pocket, handed one to Rivera, two to Jefferson.

"His hands and his ankles."

Heaving and thrashing, Prescott fought once more against Blancanales on top of him, his throat making a high, whining sound. Blancanales slammed Prescott's head into the rotted carpet again and again until Prescott stopped struggling. He lay still, his face in the ancient filth of the carpet, gagging.

Rivera studied the plastic loop. He determined how

it worked, then cinched it tight around the prisoner's wrists. Jefferson, too, linked one strand to the next to secure Prescott's ankles.

"Here," Blancanales motioned to Jefferson. "One foot on his neck while I search him. Don't break it."

As Blancanales went through the lawyer's pockets, Jefferson put a jogging shoe on the lawyer's neck. He bore down and joked. "Well, imagine this, Bobby. You had me all set up. Sold me out, sold out the Riveras, sold out your country. Must've been a real laugh in Buckley's office, listening to me talk, watching me shake while I looked outside at the goons. And all the time I was talking to a goon." He pressed his foot down slightly.

Prescott gasped.

Blancanales found the folded map. He looked at the red-ink directions. He passed the map to Jefferson.

"You know Los Angeles? What sort of neighborhood is that?"

Reading the names of the freeways and boulevards, glancing at the position of the Los Angeles International Airport to double-check, Jefferson shook his head.

"No one lives there. Not there. I did free-lance background on gang punks because I speak Spanish and look like a ghetto punk. I went there. Looks like a nuke zone, *nadaland* . . . 'land of nothing' . . . that's where he was taking the Riveras! There, man, there!"

Motioning Jefferson aside, Blancanales resumed the interrogation. He held the map in front of Prescott's face.

"Are they waiting there? Answer me."

"I'll sue you for everything you have—"

Blancanales drove a fist into the side of the lawyer's head. Prescott groaned. He strained against the plastic handcuffs, finally went limp again.

"You threatened me," Blancanales told him, his voice calm, quiet. "Don't do that. Understand your position. You are a prisoner. Your life depends on your cooperation. You are very lucky my partner, Ironman is not here. You give him some chickenshit threat like a lawsuit and he will *take you apart*. He'll do it. Or maybe I'll do it."

Blancanales stabbed a finger at the red-ink address. "We've got the location. Now I'm giving you the opportunity to help us. Help us, and you go to a clean, safe prison. Don't help us and . . . Floyd, *qué piensas?*"

"What do we do to him?"

"Use your imagination." Blancanales gave Jefferson a wink.

"I don't have to imagine anything," the reporter said. "I saw the pictures of the Rivera boy—"

Prescott thrashed and jerked at his restraints.

Blancanales smiled and nodded. "This guy saw the pictures, too. But I got a better idea than that. We're going to give you to the *Blancos*. A one-way ticket to El Salvador. And a letter of thanks for helping us wipe out *Los Guerreros Blancos*—"

Prescott screamed. Blancanales punched his head again.

"Quiet."

"Little Bobbie Prescott's afraid of that." Jefferson laughed.

"Now will you cooperate?" Blancanales asked him.

"I was to take...the family there. Madrano's waiting. With his men. I don't know anything else. Nothing else."

"Where are they waiting? Is it a house? A warehouse?"

"They only...they gave me that map."

Blancanales heard paper rustling. He saw Jefferson returning his sawed-off shotgun to its shopping-bag camouflage. From astride Prescott, Blancanales shook his head.

"You're staying here, Floyd."

"What? You'll need me. There'll be an army of goons waiting for you."

"No."

"Ask the other guys. They know I'm qualified."

"I'm not saying you're not qualified. You proved yourself the first night. But you're staying here. Don't argue. No compromises. You stay."

"Sheeee—it, man! I'm the one they tried to kill. And Marquez was my friend. He got me started when I left college. I owe it to him—"

"And what if a bullet takes you? Mr. Holt wanted to have you testify to Congress, right? Now you've got something to talk about. You stay here, then you go to Congress, then you go to court when Prescott goes on trial. It's your duty. Let us do ours."

"Sheee—it...."

Señor Rivera spoke. "Floyd, I would feel much safer if you stay. We only have a knife. You have a gun. Please stay. You are brave, but I have only a knife to defend my wife and daughters. *Por favor*."

"Of course, sir. I will. I understand. Okay, Rosario? I stay."

Blancanales nodded, resumed his interrogation of Prescott by seizing the back of his shirt collar and pulling tight as he leaned forward to speak into Prescott's ear. "Now, how many men?"

"I saw... five or six or eight. Many men in a room. They had those machine guns made in Israel. Like the Secret Service carries."

"Good." Blancanales stood. He glared down at Prescott. "Up. We're going—"

"No! They'll torture me. They'll—"

"Forget what they'll do. Think about what *we'll* do."

GALLUCCI CURSED as he watched the broad-shouldered Hispanic escort Prescott from the hotel. The man took the car keys from Prescott and opened the driver's door. He checked the interior before shoving Prescott inside. Then the Hispanic went to the passenger side and opened the door.

The receiver in Gallucci's car blared out noise again, the slamming of the doors, the jingling of keys, voices.

"What's this radio for?" a deep voice demanded.

"Captain Madrano gave it to me. In case I got lost, I could contact them."

Squeaks. Then the rustling of papers. Then a slam as the "specialist" closed the glove-compartment door. The minimike transmitted only muffled sounds and the vibrations of the car's starter.

Almost two blocks away, Gallucci punched the dashboard in anger. He had no doubt Prescott had broken. He would lead the "specialists" directly to Captain Madrano. Gallucci had to set the contingency plans in motion. Warn Madrano. Get the standby hit team in motion. Then wipe out Prescott and the "specialists."

Prescott would cooperate with the Justice Department. He had to die. All of them had to die: Prescott, the "specialists," the Riveras, that high-yellow nigger Floyd Jefferson.

The situation had to be sterilized.

He pressed the transmit key of the walkie-talkie. "Calling my friend, this is the *federali*...."

Only static answered him. He repeated his transmission. "Calling my friend, this is the *federali*. Come in, important message about the girls...."

Out of range! The walkie-talkie's signal could not penetrate the steel and concrete of central Los Angeles and cross the ten or twelve miles to Captain Madrano's squad.

Starting the engine of his federal vehicle, Gallucci considered tailing Prescott and his captor. No. They might rendezvous with a squad of "specialists," or they might interrogate Prescott before attempting to arrest the Salvadorans. Gallucci's first move must be to warn Madrano and get the hit team in motion.

Gallucci waited until Prescott's Dodge pulled into the traffic of occasional cars and trucks speeding through skid row. Then he left his bureau Dodge and ran across a parking lot to a pay phone.

The Sheraton switchboard answered.

"Good morning, Sheraton Hotel."

"Room 615, please." Gallucci told the operator. He listened as the phone rang eight times.

The operator returned to the line. "There's no answer, sir. Would you like to leave a message?"

Gallucci dropped the phone and ran back to his car. Accelerating, he raced to the freeway. He had to get within the signal range of Captain Madrano's radio. Only then could Gallucci warn the Salvadoran.

Only then could they set the contingency plan of ambush and sterilization in motion.

ABLE TEAM SPED SOUTH on the Harbor Freeway, Blancanales and Prescott in the first car, Gadgets and Lyons following in the second. Lyons radioed Blancanales.

"When we get off, we give that car a complete search, agreed?"

"I searched it," Blancanales's voice answered. "It's a rental. Found only Prescott's briefcase and the walkie-talkie."

"A complete search," Lyons stressed. "The trunk, under the hood, the underside—"

"Visual and electronic," Gadgets added.

"Looking at this map," Blancanales responded, "we'll be there maybe four minutes after we leave the freeway. We're parking and then going in on foot, correct? Even if they have a D.F. on the car, they won't know it's us or even where we park. We might be late already. I don't know if we want to risk the extra ten or fifteen minutes."

"You want our arrival announced?" Lyons asked.

Gadgets took the hand-radio from Lyons. He spoke

as he maintained a one-handed seventy miles per hour, steering smoothly to glide from one lane to another through the light traffic.

"Pol, dig it. Prescott said these Nazis pay in gold. We know they use good equipment. That trick with the shielded and pulse-switched D.F. on the motor home proved it. They could have anything on that car—"

Lyons leaned to the hand-radio and added, "What about a radio-triggered bomb as a backup? Prescott goes softhearted and tries to take the Riveras away— Bang. If we can use electronic force multiplication, why not them?"

"Maybe...." Blancanales admitted.

"You're in the car, Political." Gadgets laughed. "Give it some thought...."

Blancanales sighed through the encoding and decoding electronics of the hand-radio. "You talked me into it. We'll do a quick search."

HEADING WEST on Century Boulevard, Gallucci pressed the transmit key of the walkie-talkie again. "This is *el federal*. Can you hear me?"

Words finally answered, static-blurred but audible. "Yes...we wait."

"They took Prescott."

"What?"

"They—took—Prescott."

"Who?"

"The 'specialists.' I watched them march him to the car. They may be coming."

"You said the 'specialists'? The ones who guard the Communist reporter?"

"They took Prescott. They know about you."

Static, then cursing in Spanish. "They come?"

"I don't know. If not now, soon. Time to send out your second squad. And you should get ready."

Static and laughter. "We will be ready."

IN ONLY A FEW MINUTES, Captain Madrano had reorganized his men into an ambush. He also dispatched four men to liquidate the Riveras.

Then the Salvadoran soldiers waited, concealed in the urban desolation of what had been a suburban neighborhood before bureaucrats and vandals ran wild.

Overgrown hedges and the blackened ruins of stucco houses concealed the soldiers. In the always-gray overcast of the Los Angeles night, they had both vision and concealment. Anyone arriving in an automobile would be an easy target.

The first car appeared. Captain Madrano recognized the rental Dodge Prescott had driven to the Sheraton. He shouted the command to his men:

"Fire!"

Ten Uzi submachine guns ripped the Dodge in one long maelstrom of 9mm death.

31

Leaving the freeway, Able Team had pulled into a closed service station. Security lights bathed the asphalt surrounding the sheet-metal garage in blue white glare. Wire mesh covered all the windows of the garage and station office. A body shop adjoined the gas station. Behind the chain link and razor-wire enclosing the smashed or primer-red cars, guard dogs paced.

Gadgets parked behind the blue Dodge Prescott was driving and surveyed the area, the wire-mesh station windows, the guard dogs, the boulevard of boarded-over windows and abandoned cars.

"Not a good neighborhood," he said to Lyons.

"Understatement of the year," Lyons told him. "You're in cannibal territory here."

Gadgets laughed as he took his counterelectronics wand from his equipment case. "You got a weird sense of humor, Ironman. Do all cops make jokes like that?"

"Who's joking? The world we live in, I only tell the truth. People don't believe it, so they laugh."

"The district sure looks bad," Gadgets countered as they left the car, "but it can't be *that* bad."

"Hey, Wizard, this is Lennox. There really is a gang

here called 'The Cannibals.' When I was with the LAPD, we never were able to get an informer into the club. Seems the initiation rite is—"

"You're jiving!" Gadgets passed the wand under Prescott's car.

"No jive," Lyons insisted.

Blancanales passed the car keys to Lyons. "You telling more cop jokes?"

Opening the trunk, Lyons threw the keys back to Blancanales. "No jokes," Lyons continued. "To join the gang, a punk had to murder somebody and then eat them. No jive. I am serious."

"Man, I can't believe that." Gadgets laughed. "Your arm wound's infecting your head. How is your arm, by the way."

Lyons went flat on his back and directed a flashlight beam at the undercarriage of the car. "It's cool," he said.

Gadgets searched the interior of the trunk with a flashlight and the counterelectronic wand; slamming the trunk closed, he opened the rear passenger-side door.

The wand buzzed. Gadgets swept it over the rear seat and over Prescott. The tone faded. He waved it toward the dashboard. The tone became loud. Then Blancanales opened the glove compartment. Gadgets touched the wand to the walkie-talkie. The device shrieked.

Blancanales and Gadgets glanced to one another. Gadgets signaled his partners to be silent with a finger over his lips. He pointed to the walkie-talkie, then sat in the seat and disassembled it. Lyons continued searching the undercarriage.

Headlights swept the gas station. A lowered Oldsmobile pulled up beside Able Team's cars. A tape unit blasted soul music. Red light illuminated the interior of the Olds.

Two black men—one man in a purple satin turban, the other with a vast cloud of ratted "natural" hair—looked over at the three men in the Dodge. The music cut off.

"Well, say, honkies, What you doin' on our side a' town?"

"We're just tourists," Blancanales answered. "Reading a road map."

"Got any money?" the driver—the man with the cloud of ratted hair—demanded.

Gadgets looked up as he deactivated the minimike, shook his head. Slowly, Blancanales reached under his coat.

"Keep your hand where it is, mother!" the driver shouted. The second man threw open the Olds's passenger-side door.

Lyons stood up with his silenced Colt held at assault height, his right hand braced against his gut, his left hand gripping the Colt's fold-down lever.

Glass exploded as he swept the interior of the Oldsmobile with bursts of silent .45 ACP hollowpoints. The first burst exploded the driver's head. Hunks of hairy skull plastered the inside of the shattered windshield. The second burst caught the man in the turban as he twisted in the seat to point a sawed-off double-barreled shotgun. The three slugs tore away his left arm and his jaw. A horrible whine bubbled from his devastated face as his right hand spasmed, pulling both triggers of the shotgun. His left leg disintegrated in the flash.

In motion as the first man died, Blancanales put his Beretta 93-R on line. He ripped the front seat with bursts of subsonic 9mm steel-cored slugs, ending the agony of the half-faced, maimed felon. Blancanales "killed" the headless driver again, the corpse jumping and twitching as it fell to tangle with the mangled corpse of his partner in terror.

Lyons fired two bursts into the back seat. He glanced inside, saw only the two dead men.

"Time to go!" he shouted to his partners.

Already in motion, Gadgets ran to the other car. Able Team accelerated with smoking tires. In seconds, they left the scene of sudden death far behind. They continued west on Century Boulevard. Gadgets looked over to Lyons. He broke the silence.

"One question, Ironman."

"What?"

Gadgets followed the taillights of the rental Dodge as it turned off the boulevard. Several blocks short of the location marked on the map, the two cars stopped.

Fire-gutted and vandalized houses lined the streets. Many houses had been moved from the lots, leaving only foundations where families had lived.

Blancanales threw Prescott into the back seat and cuffed his wrists and ankles behind him, linking the cuffs to pull Prescott's ankles up to his wrists.

The three warriors of Able Team assembled their weapons, and slipped into their Kevlar and steel-plate battle armor. Bandoliers crisscrossed the black armor.

The laughter of only a minute ago had gone. Now they talked quietly as they armed themselves.

"Prescott didn't have any prearranged signal," Blancanales told the others. "Not even a code on the walkie-talkie—"

"So he wouldn't freak the family," Gadgets added.

"Right," Blancanales agreed. "He was to drive up slow and the *Blancos* would take them. So they'll be waiting curbside. What I thought is we could drive up with the high beams on to blind them. Second car stays a block back, no lights. When they step out, I'll floor it."

"I'll ride shotgun," Lyons volunteered. "In the back seat, with the Atchisson, I'll have 180 degrees field of fire to the rear. Forget the windows and roof posts. I'll put down everything in the street."

"They'll scramble to chase us," Blancanales continued. "But I'll kill the lights after about a block and wait—"

"And I'll come up behind them with the Beretta," Gadgets told them. "Man! Wish I had a cassette tape of the girls and the mother and father talking in Spanish. Would have been perfect with that minimike. *El último perfecto.*"

"Too bad." By touch, Lyons checked the number of tiny MU-50G grenades in the thigh pockets of his night-black fatigues. "But it ain't a perfect world."

Blancanales put his hands on his partners' shoulders. He spoke in sober, sincerely felt words. "But we're doing what we can, right? For a better world?"

"Don't get ideological," Gadgets told him with a straight face. "I'm only doing this for a pension. Doing what they tell me, punching that time card, till the day I can retire to a life of luxury.''

The three men laughed at Gadgets's standard put-on.

A roar of auto-fire stopped their laughter.

IN THE GRAY LUMINESCENCE of the Los Angeles night, the bullet-torn Dodge lurched to a stop on flattened tires. Slugs from the Uzis of the *Guerreros Blancos* continued to hammer the pocked doors. Ricochets slammed into the stucco of the deserted houses across the street. Captain Madrano emptied his second magazine of cartridges into the driver's door, then reloaded his scorching hot Uzi.

Surveying the street, Madrano watched as his soldiers continued raking the wrecked Dodge. He had fired a total of sixty rounds into the car. Certainly, he and his soldiers had killed the ''specialists from Washington'' riding inside. He shouted out to his men:

''*¡Alto! ¡Alto!*''

The auto-fire died away. Madrano motioned for his lieutenant to check the hulk.

Zigzagging as they had taught him at Fort Bragg, the lieutenant dashed into the street. He looked into the Dodge, then flicked on a flashlight. After searching the interior with the beam, he called out to the captain:

''*¡El federal!*''

Captain Madrano left his concealment. The stink of gasoline swirled in the cool night. The flashlight's beam illuminated a sickening mass of flesh and torn clothing. Spilled intestines reeked of excrement. Vinyl and auto glass and foam plastic mixed with the gore.

What remained of the head had the face of Agent Gallucci.

Confused, not believing what had happened, Captain Madrano backed away from the car. The stink of gasoline choked him. He looked down at the asphalt. Gasoline and blood flowed from the bullet-patterned automobile. The captain grabbed the flashlight from his lieutenant and looked in again.

No corpses sprawled in the back of the Dodge. And only one body—not actually a body any longer, actually a tangled spill of body parts—covered the front seat.

Agent Gallucci.

Captain Madrano had killed Colonel Quesada's most effective North American. A North American who operated within the same agencies threatening the Families of El Salvador with investigation and indictment and slander. Though Colonel Quesada had forgiven his blunder in the mountains south of San Jose, because of the friendship of their families and their intermingled bloodlines, how could Madrano beg forgiveness for this?

Shining the flashlight down on the horror that had been a valuable informer, Madrano prepared his explanation to his father's friend. He prepared his defense as a playwright imagines a scene, the dialogue flying back and forth between the characters, the hand gestures, the drama of emphasizing his words with soft words, then shouts, then silence.

No problem. I can explain it. The North American misunderstood or disregarded instructions.

Captain Madrano had always explained away his

failures and mistakes. The students looked alike. The house numbers had been tampered with. One street looked like another. The man with the pistol and uniform had not looked like a real policeman. I'll be more careful next time. Please do not shame my father and my family because of this insignificant and forgettable error. Please, for the honor of the army, forgive me....

If the other squad succeeds in executing the Communist family, Captain Madrano thought, *all will be well.* He could hear his impassioned speech to Colonel Quesada: "Gallucci's blunder was unfortunate, but the Communists died. True, it was a quick death. It was not the justice I wanted to give them. But it is a step onward to victory of the fatherland!"

For two minutes, the men of the death squad stood in the street and waited as Captain Madrano stood motionless at the wreck, staring down at his error, mentally rehearsing the scene in which he would win the forgiveness of Colonel Quesada. The men glanced at their watches. They looked around at the darkness.

Unlike the police of San Salvador, the police of Los Angeles did not honor the extraordinary privileges of *El Ejercito de los Guerreros Blancos*. The men knew they faced arrest and a few days of jail. As their leaders had assured them, the administration would grant the squad immediate release—as in the murders of the North Americans in El Salvador—but the questions and publicity would be embarrassing.

They did not see the onrushing automobile until it neared them. For a moment, they stared.

Quietly, without lights, an automobile hurtled at

them in reverse. The Salvadoran soldiers stared at the rear bumper and rear windows of the automobile.

Doubts restrained their reflex to fire. If the automobile had raced toward them directly, the soldiers would have raised their weapons and fired instantly.

But an attack in reverse? Four of their compatriots had departed only minutes ago. Could this be their friends returning for some reason? Then they realized the automobile had a different color and manufacturer than the vehicle their compatriots drove.

The Dodge braked suddenly. As the driver slammed the transmission into forward and smoked the tires with acceleration, the rear windows exploded outward.

A deafening auto weapon boomed. Glass floated in the air, a universe of tiny red stars as the cubes of tempered glass flashed with the red muzzle-flash of a weapon sweeping the standing Salvadorans.

As the *Blancos* raised their Uzis, as men dived for the shelter of graffitied walls and trash mounds, a storm of projectiles swept them. One of the gunmen twisted in the air as a pattern of high-velocity steel balls tore through his body. Another lurched and staggered as his through-and-through wounds spurted blood. Another fell screaming, his legs collapsing backward from multiple hits that shattered his knees and his leg bones.

The car screeched away. Slugs from the *Blancos'* Uzis sought it.

An explosion boiled upward. A wave of flame enveloped the dead Gallucci's gasoline-drenched automobile. The soldiers heard a scream as Captain Madrano writhed on the asphalt in a hell of gasoline fire.

Justice by fire lit the night.

32

Flat in the back seat, Lyons snapped a safety belt around his waist as Uzi slugs hammered the Dodge. Slugs hitting the trunk lid shrieked across the sheet steel and through the interior of the car to shatter the windshield.

Behind the car, he heard the pops of 40mm grenades killing the *Blancos*. An orange flash colored the darkness.

Blancanales lay flat in the front seat, his head below the level of the car's windows. He did not steer the car. He only held the steering wheel straight as his foot kept the accelerator to the floor.

The bodywork's steel, the spare tire and the seats protected both men from the lightweight 9mm bullets. Hurtling away from the wild auto-fire of the *Blancos* at sixty miles per hour, the Dodge swerved from curb to curb on the empty street of the desolated suburb until a front wheel went up a driveway. The undercarriage scraped concrete as the car jumped the curb. Bouncing across lawns, crashing through shrubbery, the car smashed into the arson-gutted frame of a house.

Ashes and stucco and framing fell. Unsnapping his safety belt, Lyons looked around. A fire-charred wall leaned on the front and one side of the Dodge. Tangled bushes screened them from the view of the *Blancos* a block behind them.

Lyons smelled gasoline. "Pol! Out of here!"

"You need help?" Blancanales asked as he kicked a door open.

"Not me, I thought—"

"Don't think. Move. This car's about to burn."

Pushing aside boards and branches and sheets of stucco, they staggered to the lawn. Lyons scanned the street and other yards, his Atchisson on line. The gray dome of the sky cast a half-glow on the neighborhood. No one had pursued them.

The flaming hulk on the next block lit the street and house fronts. Silhouettes dashed from cover to cover. Wounded men clawed at the asphalt, pools of blood around them shimmering with flamelight.

Blancanales keyed his hand-radio. "Wizard. We're out. Which way are they moving?"

"They're not! What a crew of losers. They're panicked and screaming."

"We're on our way...."

"Make distance!" Lyons hissed. "Here comes a distraction...."

Blancanales saw Lyons point his silenced Colt at the rear end of the Dodge. The jacketed slug sparked off the concrete foundation of the wrecked house, then the leaking gasoline roared.

Thrashing through shrubbery, they left the flames behind them. The gas tank exploded, a fireball churning into the night. They dropped low as the street went bright with the orange light.

Two *Blancos* ran from the wild firefight. The moment of rising flame illuminated their sweat-shining, panicked faces. One man limped badly, his strides awkward. The second man ran past the first, made no effort to help his compatriot as the man's wounded leg buckled.

The wounded man called out as he struggled to rise from the street. "Armando! Armando, *ayudeme...* *ayude....*"

Armando did not turn or slow in his sprint.

Lyons glanced to Blancanales. "Prisoners?"

"We'll leave them for the police." Blancanales let his borrowed CAR rifle hang on his shoulder as he sighted his Beretta.

Bursts of slugs tore Armando's legs, a steel-cored 9mm shattering one knee, another low-powered 9mm breaking the shinbone of the other leg. Lyons scored only one hit on the falling death-squadder, but the merciless .45 ACP hollowpoint exploded through the man's thigh, the expanding disk of spinning metal decelerating in a microsecond to liberate 400 foot-pounds of shock force. Blood and muscle and bone sprayed from an exit wound three inches in diameter.

The limping man behind Armando took the next bursts, a .45 ACP ripping away a foot and breaking the other leg. Nine millimeter slugs from Blancanales's selective-fire pistol punched through his knees.

Screaming, moaning, calling out in incomprehensible Spanish, the men thrashed on the sidewalk. Blancanales pulled lengths of prepared nylon cord from his pocket and started toward the wounded *Blancos*. Lyons jerked him back.

"Leave them. We don't owe them any tourniquets.

The more blood they lose, the less chance they'll shoot the sheriffs when they get here—which will be in about one minute!''

Sprinting ahead, Lyons dodged from shadow to shadow. At the corner house, he dashed up porch steps and stood behind a brick column. Over the sights of his Atchisson, he surveyed the scene on the next block.

No *Blancos* exposed themselves. No auto-fire broke the sudden quiet. A scream rose, faded to a whine.

Blancanales joined him. As Lyons squinted into the shadows of a driveway—did he see a man moving, a car door opening—he heard Blancanales whisper into his hand-radio.

''We're on the southwest corner. Where are they?''

A 40mm grenade cracked. No auto-fire answered. Blancanales whispered into the radio again. ''Wizard!''

''Wait a second!'' Gadgets answered. The radio went silent for a moment.

Lyons watched a driveway where the overspreading branches of a tree created a pocket of darkness. He saw a shadow move. Could it be only the rising and falling flames from the burning car?

Gadgets's voice returned. ''Dudes, I'm all tangled up in wires. I'm monitoring three radios and trying to kill people, too. I got to get an assistant—''

''What do you see?'' Blancanales interrupted.

''I don't see anything. But I'm hearing things. The goon squad's forming up for a breakout, so watch out.''

Bracing the Atchisson against the column, the auto-shotgun's sights on line with the tree's night shadow,

Lyons reached out with his left hand and pulled Blancanales's radio close enough to transmit his whisper.

"You got the scanner on?"

"Most definitely! Sheriffs' copter on the way. And they're assembling superior firepower. They know they got something *bad* happ'nin' in dis *nadaland*."

"Talk English, will you!" Lyons told him.

"You English? I'm not. Why should I talk that talk?" Gadgets answered.

An engine revved. Lyons saw a car accelerate from the darkness of the driveway. He did not fire.

"Hold off, Politician," Lyons cautioned his partner. The burning hulk in the center of the street blocked any straight-line escape. Keeping his right hand on the Atchisson's pistol grip, his eyes on the car, Lyons found the uppermost pouch on his bandolier. He pulled out a seven-round magazine of one-ounce slugs.

A 40mm grenade missed the car, plopped inside the house. Then Gadgets fired three-shot bursts of 5.56mm slugs.

A side window shattered. The driver whipped a hard right turn, putting the flaming Dodge between his car and the unseen rifleman, then raced for the end of the block.

Fishtailing through the intersection in a floored-accelerator left turn, the escaping *Blancos* hurtled directly into Lyons's and Blancanales's weapons. In one long explosion of 12-gauge fury, Lyons full-autoed seven rounds of high-velocity steel through the windshield. He dropped the empty magazine and jammed in the magazine of slugs.

Blancanales scythed the interior with a line of alternating military and hollowpoint 5.56mm, all thirty slugs tearing through the interior.

As the careering, out-of-control car failed to hold its high-speed left turn through the intersection, Lyons pounded the car with semi-auto steel-cored slugs. A door panel collapsed inward, gore sprayed from the far side. The car passed only ten feet away. Lyons snapped two more slugs through the shot-out back window as the car full of dead and dying *Guerreros Blancos* crashed into the house.

Lyons jumped from the porch. He crouched and aimed at the gas-tank filler cap. The slug tore through the sheet metal. He aimed the last slug lower, fired into the gas tank.

No flames came. Pocketing the emptied magazine, he reloaded. Left-handed, he took an MU-50G mini-grenade from his thigh pocket. Not taking his right hand from his Atchisson's pistol grip, he stuck a finger through the cotter pin's ring, jerked it free.

A sound came from inside the car. A groaning, a gasping. A wounded *Blanco* tried to form words. Lyons called out:

"Does it hurt? Don't you like it?" He pitched the grenade under the wreck. "Go back to where you came from!"

As flames and choking black smoke rose into the gray night of Los Angeles, Lyons, Blancanales and Gadgets sped away.

33

Floyd Jefferson waited in the dark. As a game to keep himself awake, he listened to the sounds of the old hotel and the city outside. He heard the raspy breathing of Señor Rivera, asleep in a chair a few steps away, the long butcher knife clutched in his hand. The señora and the three girls slept in the bed, their arms around one another, the quiet sound of their breathing like distant waves. One of the girls moved and the old springs of the bed squeaked.

Startling awake, Señor Rivera straightened in his chair. The glow from the window revealed his look to Floyd. Floyd lifted his left hand in a mock salute. His right hand remained closed around the slick-tape grip of the sawed-off shotgun.

Letting his hearing travel the hotel, Floyd listened to the sounds of flushing toilets and faint voices. The solid brick walls blocked most of the hotel sounds. But outside the window, the noises of Los Angeles created a three-dimensional texture of late-night life.

A siren wailed. Floyd listened as it approached, growing louder, reverberating in the stone and glass canyons of the downtown boulevards, then fading as it continued away. He heard voices from the street, the screeching of tires, a blasting car radio.

Silence came, all the other sounds inexplicably absent. Small claws skittered on the steel of the fire escape outside. Shuddering, Jefferson looked toward the window. Rats.

He did not need to see them to imagine them. After five nights without sleep, the sounds of their claws created glowing rats on a giant fire escape in the theater of his mind.

Cool, kid. Be cool. You got worse than rats out there. Maybe. If his friends the "specialists" did their number, the goons would *not* be out there.

Five days? Had it been that long? Two nights in Miami. The night before he and Mr. Holt planned to fly to Washington. The night in that traitor Prescott's office. And tonight.

A few hours' sleep in Miami. No sleep the night before Washington—thought I'd be making international news, couldn't sleep thinking about that! No sleep the night at Prescott's, not with the goon squad waiting. And tonight.

Maybe he could sleep on the plane. When Pol and Ironman and Wizard get back, everyone gets on a plane north, finds a place to hide out while they splash the newspapers with this story!

What a story. Jefferson looked at Señor Rivera. A proud, hard-working man. His grandfather a *ladino* peddler. Traveled around selling things. His father a shopkeeper, kept his little store open dawn to midnight to pay his son's way through college. Señor Rivera made it big. Lawyer, mayor of his town. Made the mistake of thinking the government really wanted land reform, to stop the Communist revolution by letting the farm workers and sharecroppers buy the land they had worked all their lives. An idealist. Land reform is the law, therefore he types up the forms and passes out the titles.

One bullet for him.

The señora and the girls. Four bullets for them.

Maybe even a bullet or two for me, thought Jefferson. Oh, boy. And I pay for it.

Horror-images flashed inside Jefferson's head. Stop thinking about that!

Tapping his feet on the linoleum and humming an old Puerto Rican song his mother sang years before, Jefferson stroked the shotgun. The cold steel comforted him.

They can kill me, but they can't hack me. At least, not while I'm alive. They won't do to me like they did to Señor Rivera's son.

Gouge out his eyes, hack up his body, carve off his balls and choke him to death with them. Choking to death on his own flesh.

The images came out of the darkness at Jefferson and he startled awake. Señor Rivera shook the young man. His face floated in the darkness as the Salvadoran whispered, "You slept...."

"Ah, thanks. No good...can't sleep. No way. Not until we know...."

"Morning will come soon. Then we go to another place."

Jefferson shook his head. "No, sir. By morning it's over. One way or another."

"Perhaps."

Glancing at his watch, Jefferson saw that only forty-five minutes had passed since Prescott knocked on the door of the other room.

Talk about the long night of the soul.

Knocking broke the silence. The reporter bolted to his feet. His sneakers silent on the linoleum, he crept to the door. He had to listen for voices. If his friends had returned, if they had already eliminated the *Guerreros Blancos*, they would return to an empty room—because a minute after Blancanales had escorted Prescott downstairs, Jefferson, in a flash of inspiration, had run down to the desk clerk. If Prescott knew the address and room number of the Riveras, the *Blancos* did also. Twenty dollars bought another room for the Riveras. With a bed. And without the stinking carpet.

Don't want the Team to come back and find us all gone. A paranoid nightmare!

Putting his ear against the door, Jefferson listened. By force of habit, his right index finger stroked the not-quite-closed bolt of the shotgun. "Unlocked Carry," Pol had called it.

A door closed with a slam. Jefferson heard voices speaking Spanish. He waited, listening with his ear to the door.

Couldn't be the Team, Jefferson realized. They talked English. To each other. Except for Wizard. He talked jive.

More voices. A voice whined in English. Jefferson recognized the voice as that of the desk clerk, a fat little man who talked about "excellent" television programs.

In the silence of the room, both Jefferson and Señor Rivera heard the faint creaking of hallway floorboards as several persons approached their room. Jefferson looked to Señor Rivera. Then he looked to the señora and the three girls.

Señor Rivera went to the bed. Shaking his wife and daughters, he woke them. He whispered instructions as a voice whined in the hallway.

Jefferson stepped away from the door. He pressed his back against the wall. With a thousand bedspring squeaks, the señora and the three girls left the bed and crowded into the bathroom.

The desk clerk whined. "This is the room—don't—"

Metal smashed flesh. As Jefferson panic-flexed his arms to close the sawed-off shotgun's bolt, a foot kicked the door.

The hallway's dim light silhouetted a broad-shouldered young soldier with an Uzi submachine gun. Muzzle-flash lighting the tiny room, the auto-fire reports deafening, the *Blanco* tore the bed apart with high-velocity 9mm slugs.

Slugs shattered the window and hammered the walls.

He stepped in, waving the Uzi from side to side.

Putting the 12-gauge bore against the *Blanco*'s chest, Jefferson fired. Heart and lung tissue sprayed the hallway.

A second soldier stepped forward, his Uzi flashing.

In his panic and adrenaline courage, Jefferson did not feel the bullets. He pumped the shotgun's action and fired point-blank into the gut of the second man. Then he pumped the action again.

The room seemed distant, as if all the walls had suddenly retreated. Jefferson coughed blood. But still he stood.

Staggering, placing one foot deliberately in front of the other, he looked into the hall. He saw only the desk clerk's body on the ancient, filthy carpet.

Something tore Jefferson's head. He heard the shots as he fell back into the room. He did not feel himself fall, he still gripped the shotgun, but he no longer stood.

"*¡Mi hijo!*" Jefferson heard Señor Rivera call out. A sheet of flame seemed to sear his vision. He realized he lay on his back, his head against one of the bedframe legs. The light from the hallway blinded him. He squinted against it.

A silhouette appeared. Movement and grunting. Jefferson saw Señor Rivera pull the butcher knife from the torso of a third *Blanco*, then try to drive the knife in again.

But the wounded *Blanco* shoved Rivera away. As his life faded, as if in slow motion, Jefferson saw the *Blanco* aiming his Uzi to kill the father of the children hiding in the bathroom.

Save the children. . . .

Jefferson pointed the shotgun at the *Blanco* with his left hand and forced his right hand to close on the trigger.

A flash.

No silhouette.

Crying.

Darkness.

Voices and hands. A light. Blood in his mouth. The voices of the Team. Pol, Wizard, the crazy one. The faces and hands of the girls, touching him. The girls he had saved.

A siren and the blue white lights of Los Angeles streaking through his vision.

He would be saved...!

FOR THE TEAM—for Pol, Wizard and the crazy one—Quesada joined Unomundo as living proof that a bizarre new Third Reich was continuing to grow in Central America.

But that was a job for tomorrow....

```
*** CODE TWO ***
FROM JD/WASH 150800E
TO BROGNOLA/STONY MAN *** IMMEDIATE ***
PURSUANT TO STONYMAN REQUEST FBI ATTEMPTED
ARREST OF COLONEL QUESADA MIAMI RESIDENT
SALVADORAN NATIONAL X HOWEVER SUBJECT FLED
BEFORE ARRIVAL OF OFFICERS X WHEREABOUTS
UNKNOWN X QUERY FORWARDED EMBASSY SAN
SALVADOR X JUSTICE DEPARTMENT REMINDS
STONYMAN THERE IS NO EXTRADITION TREATY
BETWEEN UNITED STATES AND EL SALVADOR X JD
***
```

ABLE TEAM

AN EXECUTIONER SERIES

8 Army of Devils

MORE GREAT ACTION
COMING SOON!

When frenzied incidents of brutality escalate in Los Angeles, they are traced to the slums—and a new drug.

Addicts hungry for "China Blue"—a synthetic drug one hundred times more powerful than any known narcotic—terrorize the city. Gangs attack homes, rove the freeways to kill commuters. Gunmen besiege police stations, decimate narco strike-squads with automatic weapons and rocket-propelled grenades.

Only Able Team has the firepower—and the guts—to confront the crazies and expose a plot to attack the U.S. with a proxy army of brutal zombies.

Watch for new Able Team titles
wherever paperbacks are sold.